DOG DAZE OF FALL

The Dog Tail Detective Series

MARYANNE VANDYKE

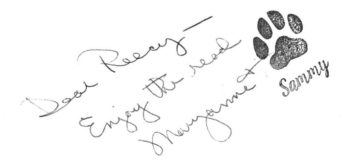

Dear Reecy —
Enjoy the read
Maryanne
Sammy

Acknowledgments

I'd like to thank the many people who helped make this book possible through their generosity by providing advice and encouragement. Without all of you, Sam would never have shared his memoir.

Laura Logsdon Buchanan, my darling daughter, who used her organizational skills to critique and inspire me along the path to stories end.

Leona and Jack (Harry) Applegate, loveable characters in real life, as well as in this novel.

Gayle and Paul Short who lent their name and editing to Sam's story.

Barbara Cassell, Creative Writing Instructor, Smyrna Senior Activity Center, whose editing inspired me.

Fran Dunne, Director of Senior Activity Center of Smyrna, Tennessee whose vision of creativity manifests itself in the various activities afforded all members.

Gail Tucker, owner of Liliya Vita Black Russian Kennels, Nashville, Tennessee who shared valuable information about the Black Russian Breed.

Members: Senior Activity Center of Smyrna, Tennessee and Newcomers of Rutherford County who encouraged and supported Sam's journey.

Smyrna, Tennessee, Police Department who answered my questions and gave insight into several scenes.

Michele Jones, AIW Press, who bound hours of work into a neat green package.

And, finally, to Nickolas and his human mother, Pam, who shared his puppy quirks and inspired me to include him as Sammy's new doggie pal.

If you pick up a starving dog and make him prosperous, he will not bite you.
This is the principal difference between a dog and a man.
~ Mark Twain

***

ISBN-13:978-0-578-64903-0

Prologue

Explosion Rocks Memphis River Port
David Kin
Memphis Commercial Times
USA TODAY NETWORK – Tennessee

An explosion, yesterday, July 28, 5:45 CST, rocked the Memphis River Port off the pier of President's Island. The Coast Guard and Memphis Police Marine units were immediately dispatched to the scene. In the blast, a cruiser owned by Izzie and Hannah DeLisle was destroyed.

According to Memphis police, Izzie DeLisle and her dog were on the boat but escaped the blast by swimming to shore. Both were treated by the Memphis Fire Department Paramedics and released. Jessie DeLisle, uncle of the DeLisle sisters, who was on the boat at that time, has not been seen nor has his body recovered.

Police investigators, at the time of this report, are baffled by the cause of this violent explosion. Authorities were hesitant to speculate on the blast, saying only that it was caused by some type of high-order device. Police cordoned off a three-square block area, blocking traffic and crowds of spectators who came to look in the afternoon drizzle.

Due to the swift current of the Mississippi River, much of the evidence has been swept downstream. Residents in regions south of Memphis are asked to be on high alert for debris and possible human remains.

Chapter 1

The lawyer scratched his bald head above the two remaining hairs which sprouted directly above his left ear. His wire rimmed glasses pushed back in place, he continued reading.

"In conclusion, 'To my beloved Miss Daisy, for her years of companionship, trust and unconditional love, I leave a trust fund in her name in the amount of two hundred thousand as well as the total sum of my estate. To care for and guide her through her final years I appoint Isabelle (Izzie) DeLisle as her guardian. As guardian, Ms. DeLisle shall have full control over monies in Miss Daisy's name with all decisions made in use and disposition of said monies. She shall pay herself a monthly stipend of one-thousand dollars for this service. Upon Miss Daisy's death, all and any monies shall then become the property of said Isabelle (Izzie) DeLisle to be shared equally with her sister, Hannah DeLisle."

Izzie leaned forward in the oak captain's chair and gasped, her hands flew to her face covering her gaping mouth. Her hazel eyes were open wide, her eyebrows raised.

I'd laid quietly beside Daisy on the smooth varnished floor of the Hale Law Firm for the will-reading ceremony. We'd gone there with

Momma to the reading of our neighbor, Mr. Cohen's, will. I should introduce myself. My name is Samuel Dekyi DeLisle although Confidence could be my middle name. I am a handsome, grey, eighteen-pound Shih Tzu possessing a great mental capacity for solving crimes. My Shih Tzu Tibetan ancestors can be traced back many centuries. Although I was named American style with a surname, Dekyi was bestowed on me at birth by my sweet Momma many years ago. Dekyi means blissful and happy.

I have always been that kind of pup, blissful and happy, seeing no reason to ruffle my fur over circumstances which might bug others. The only bug that bothers me is an occasional flea. Those little rascals are common on the walking paths around Tom Lee Park along Riverside Drive in Memphis, Tennessee, my hometown.

I lived with my sweet Momma, Izzie, in an old warehouse turned into eight up-scale lofts by Izzie's deceased father twenty-five years ago. Our warehouse borders the mighty Mississippi River. I could not rationalize any idea why a river was called mighty, but if my Momma says it is mighty, then it must be so. I've heard Momma say the city of Memphis was founded in 1819 by Andrew Jackson, John Overton, and James Winchester. It was named after the ancient capital of Egypt on the Nile River. I liked to walk along its riverbank whiffing its funky fishy smell.

My Memphis rested along the mighty river with lovely gardens running alongside it. In the Spring, bright red azaleas bloomed along the river's walking paths under majestic magnolia trees. In the courtyard of our building, the sweet-scented azaleas provided the best bushes for me to use when I answered nature's call. Little Daisy preferred the open grass.

Miss Daisy had lived with us for the past month after the murder of our neighbor, Mr. Cohen. At the will-reading ceremony my ears went on alert when I heard the man with the wire-rimmed glasses read about my Sweet Momma's responsibilities. With that burst of knowledge, I realized Miss Daisy was to become a permanent member of our family. To be truthful with you, I'd never put together any positive thoughts about having a sibling of any gender but what could I do? Without us she would be homeless. So, I accepted my fate and future with a sister-dog.

Our lives changed forever that crisp fall day in the office of attorney Hale. If my memory serves me right, I was, in human years, eight. Daisy was twelve.

Chapter 2

A blast of cool air hit my nose when Sweet Momma, Miss Daisy and I left the lawyers office. Daisy and I jumped into our doggie car seats when Momma opened the car door. She was strict about putting us in them unless I could hop into the back-window space first. That day she fastened us in and got behind the steering wheel for the drive home. Her fingers trembled as she gripped the steering wheel with one hand. With the other she rubbed the nape of her neck, a touch she did when she experienced something wrong or if she was tense because of a problem.

Momma drove into the garage under the eight warehouse apartments we call home on Riverside Drive. Daisy and I ran from the garage straight to the courtyard. Momma tightly held our leashes. She sprinted to keep up with us. Fallen leaves from the mammoth oaks crunched under my paws. Their musty smell told me fall was here. I finished my business in lickety-split time, while Daisy smelled every bush in our courtyard before deciding to leave her mark in the grass.

This unnerving habit of Daisy's, I soon learned, would not improve in the months to come. Finally, she finished her nature-call and we followed Momma to the elevator for our ride to our loft. When we reached the fourth floor, I dashed from the elevator leaving Daisy behind.

I was eager to see my friend, Buddy, waiting in our loft for my news. I dog-spoke him a summary of what I'd learned at Mr. Hales office. We decided to accept the new family member given we had no other choice.

Fate, through our deceased neighbor Mr. Cohen, had given me a sister-dog. She would soon be dubbed Princess Daisy, due more to her attitude than her recently gained wealth.

Buddy, who had been my dog friend for years, gave her a sniff then went back to his usual spot to conduct his normal pastime, sleeping. He slept and snored much of day until it was GO time. GO was the very best word we guys knew. The sound of it could mean riding in Izzie's car or Jake's jeep peering out our back window watching for a soon-to-be adventure.

Buddy, Jake's chocolate lab, a muscular dog of ninety pounds, preferred the jeep while I preferred to ride and see the world from the back window of Izzie's Cadillac. Even if she put me in my doggie car seat, I still preferred Izzie's car to Jake's jeep. No matter which car we rode in, Buddy tried to stick his head out the window. Slobbers flew everywhere and he always got a reprimand from Jake. Buddy was gentle but stubborn. He never learned that window peeking was a bad habit that would get him in trouble.

Jake, sometimes called Mr. Squeeze by Izzie, began to play a different role in our lives after the boat explosion two years ago. Sweet Momma and I bravely jumped off her cruiser into the river before the time of the explosion. We swam the Mississippi to shore, dripping wet, scared speech-less. Izzie doesn't dog-speak. When we were safe on shore, Jake, who swam out to assist us, shared the information he had tried to tell Izzie for the past week.

He disclosed the news to Izzie they were not related, not even half brother-sister as they grew up believing. His mother revealed this in a letter to him on the day she married his real father, Guido Rocco.

From that scary, rainy day two years ago, Izzie's and Jake's love bloomed.

Many times, I watched him stare at Izzie. His fixed gaze sometimes contained a flirtatious wink or a silent kiss. I sometimes got one of his winks, but never a silent kiss. We four became a family. Sweet Momma Izzie, Jake, Buddy, and me. Now we were a family of five. Be happy for small things was my motto even if it did include Princes Daisy.

One big thing that made my heart hum with happiness was being the near-constant companion to my sweet Momma. Since my puppy days I could read her thoughts. I knew her joyful and not so joyful expressions, always doing my best by a nudge to her leg or by a tilt of my head to let her know I listened to her.

Have I told you about Izzie's hair? It flowed just past her shoulders, an auburn color, like a mud puddle after a heavy Tennessee rain. I guess it's about the color of Buddy—chocolate brown. When she pulled it back, little curls formed around her face and her neck. I looked at her hair and I was happy. It shone like the top of Lake Horn, glimmering in the moon light.

Chapter 3

I thought about Momma a lot. On the morning in question I needed to explain to Buddy the extent of the lawyer's meeting, what we had experienced at Mr. Hale's office. Sweet Momma and Daisy stepped off the elevator, following me into the loft. After a tight hug and what was, as far as I was concerned, too long a kiss to Jake, Izzie filled him in on the lawyer's meeting.

Jake rubbed his short-cropped black beard and showed the same look of surprise I'd seen on Izzie's face. She poured herself a glass of sweet tea, a liquid many Southerners drink both summer and winter, and picked up her cell phone.

"Hello, Hannah. Can you talk? You remember it was a month yesterday since Mr. Cohen's murder? This morning was the reading of his will. You'll never believe what happened at the lawyer's office. Well, yes, I did take Miss Daisy, and Sammy as well, just as I was instructed by Mr. Hale's secretary.

"Hannah, Mr. Cohen left his entire estate to Daisy under my guardianship. Can you believe it? I always considered him a close friend. You remember he was always ready with a story about Daddy when the two of them were young. But this? Never in a million, and I mean million, oh, wow, a million years would I have expected this. Mr. Hale, the attorney, explained he owned several properties, was part owner in a laundromat, and owner in a large dog breeding business in Germantown.

Mr. Hale is the executor and will handle the businesses. I am to sell his loft, care for Daisy, and take a thousand dollars a month for my service. She will be in my custody until her death at which time you and I will inherit the remainder of his estate."

The phone was silent.

"Hannah, did you hear me, what I just said?"

Hannah was on speaker phone. I heard her say, "Sorry. I'm stunned. What a generous man. Daisy is lucky to have been so loved. And, what about us being Daisy's beneficiaries." Hannah continued. Hey, I'm in town today. If you have some time I could come by. I have some good news to share."

"Sure, come on over." Izzie replied.

Buddy and I were rolling on our backs, legs straight up in the air, when I heard a knock. As is my duty, I rolled over and ran to greet the person knocking.

Hannah rushed in and gave her sister a tight hug, giving me a short pat as she walked toward the taupe sectional. "I've been thinking as I drove over. I may have a super idea for the loft. Patrick has been offered a position here in Memphis. The position requires we move here from Nashville. I've been so excited. We found out a few days ago, but I wanted to wait and tell you in person. Won't it be wonderful to live in the same city, together again? If we bought the loft, we could be neighbors. We're also eager to start a family. Wouldn't it be great to live close by?'

"Are you sure you're not just looking for a handy babysitter when that time comes?" Izzie laughed as she sat down and tucked her legs under her.

They talked and giggled, as those sisters did. It was clear to me, as I listened, it would be the perfect place for Hannah and Patrick to live. This was the month of October and according to Hannah, Patrick would be teaching in Memphis in a couple months. After much discussion, they decided the loft would be deeded to Hannah.

You may not know that since I was a puppy, Hannah, Izzie's older sister, lived in Nashville with her husband. Patrick, who was a professor at Meharry Medical College, would soon be teaching at the University of Tennessee Health Science Center.

The sisters talked every day and laughed a lot, more so if their mother Olivia had been up to some of her craziness, which she did with fair regularity. Hannah was a younger model of her mother, sharing her mother's wavy blonde hair and her tall, stately manner. Their physical appearance was the same, not their personalities.

Mother Olivia, a tall, willowy blonde in her mid-fifties, still polished and gracious, still the Southern beauty, now had a few deep frown lines. Too many nightcaps were beginning to show on her porcelain skin. She had been a widow since their daddy's murder twenty-two years ago. It was known by only a few, her true love had never been her husband, but was really her husband's brother, Jessie.

Olivia's hobbies were playing Mah Jongg and shopping. Izzie said many times Olivia excelled at the second more than the first.

Once during one of my puppy adventures around Olivia's home I discovered her closet. I was amazed to find tasty leather shoes and boots to practice my teething. There were also some long leather straps, Momma called them belts. I tugged and pulled until the whole rack fell to the floor. I grabbed a brown one and shook it as I ran through her bedroom. It wiggled behind me like a scary snake.

While Momma chased me, Olivia screamed, "Get that puppy out of my bedroom. I declare, he's ruined my beautiful belt from Santa Fe." It was great fun day. I remember it like it was yesterday.

Here's another one of those human words I find unusual. Momma said Olivia's belts were of the finest leather to wear around her waist. I remember Uncle Jessie, before he disappeared in the explosion, was said to belt a good song. I wondered, then and still do to this day, how someone could wear something around their waist, then sing it. Sometimes even my special deepest dog-think did not produce an answer.

Sorry, my mind wandered.

Izzie and Hannah were still sitting on the tweedy sectional, talking, when I came out of my dog-thinking mood.

"What about your Masquerade party scheduled for this coming Friday?"

Izzie laughed, "Yes, the costume Halloween Party is still on. Having a new dog in the family could never change our plans for a party. I forgot to tell you. Mother called. She wanted to bring a guest. I bet you she doesn't mess up her costume bobbing for apples. I'll look for you and Patrick around noon to help with the decorations."

"Okay. Don't forget we're bringing the BBQ and some carved pumpkins," Hannah said.

"I'll need to hurry and find heiress Daisy a costume before then," said Izzie. "She's such a miss-priss doggie. She'll definitely need a special princess outfit, perhaps a pink tutu would suit her."

"Does Sam play rough with her?"

"Oh, no, he's been very nice to her this past month, even let her sleep next to him. His gesture stopped her whimpering. She appears to be settled in now, romps and plays with Buddy and Sam. I admit, she has some bizarre behaviors, but I can put up with her, now that I know she's an heiress."

Buddy and I were not sure why she was an heiress because of our friend's tragic death, but if my sweet Momma said so, then it must be true.

In my puppy years I doubted Momma like any pup would, until one day while we were crossing a street. I was wearing my new red quilted parka, thinking I was the smartest looking puppy ever, when Izzie shouted "stop". A firetruck came whizzing by, its deafening sirens blaring. Right then I learned she knew what she was talking about and began to pay more attention to her instructions.

One time not long after that incident, I found an overturned trash can in the garage. Many times, when we were walking Momma would say "don't eat that" and I listened. But, on that day smells from the tossed-out chicken made my tummy growl. The fried chicken smell was hard to resist, and, after all, it was food our neighbors ate. Couldn't be bad? Right? Wrong. My tummy cramped, and I whimpered until we went to see my veterinarian, Dr. Goody. According to Momma, four hundred dollars later, I was better. Now in my mature years I remember my puppy actions and know Momma always told me the truth.

So, those were the reasons I didn't question Momma when she spoke of Miss Daisy as being an heiress. I believed her.

Chapter 4

Hannah left. Momma and Jake went to shop for a costume the Princess could wear to their masked party. I snuggled down against my green turtle with Daisy leaning against my back.

My muscles relaxed and I began to drift off. In a flash, I awoke and started to think about Mr. Cohen being murdered across the hall from us. Momma said Mr. Cohen's death was from a brutal beating. Everything she saw as she walked through the loft indicated a cruel death. She told us she followed a messy trail of blood to find him at the far end of the hall in his bathtub, an oily rag and a poker chip wedged in his mouth.

She stood, rubbing the nape of her neck—her nervous habit. Then she did her nurse thing and realized he was dead. She said it also took four shots to kill him after a baseball bat was used on his legs. From the state of the apartment, it was obvious he struggled. It surprised me he would ever fight back. I'd experienced many playdates with Daisy horsing around on his floor without him ever correcting us.

Through the years we rode the elevator with them, he was quiet-spoken and friendly. My impression of him being a gentleman, not a fighter, was very wrong. I thought I'd developed a nose for understanding humans. As this tragedy unfolded I learned, contrary to my belief in my superb nose smeller, I was wrong about many things about Mr. Cohen and his lifestyle. For one thing, from my viewpoint, I'd thought him a tall man, but seeing him stretched out in his bathtub I realized I was wrong.

He was not nearly as tall as Jake. Mr. Cohen was only as tall as the bookcase in the hall, the one Momma always ran into. He maintained great posture and stood erect like a policeman I once saw on one of my favorite Perry Mason episodes. Mr. Cohen constantly snapped his suspenders which forced me to wonder if he was nervous or if he was losing his pants. At the age of sixty, his nearly white hair receded on both sides. He was pleasant enough and adored little Daisy, whom I might add was, though much-loved, a spoiled-rotten ten-pound Shih Tzu.

You wonder why I know he was sixty? Before he left on his trip, he'd thrown a grand party for himself and Miss Daisy announcing he was sixty and she twelve. They shared the same birthday, September fourteenth. We three dogs were at the party as well as Sabbath, the Doberman from the second floor. We ate round cakes made from the finest ground liver and carrots. Momma said they were eating pate' and so were we. Pate' was a new word to me, one I soon learned to enjoy. Miss Daisy and I savored each bite while Buddy and Sabbath hastily gulped three or four each with no tummy ache after. So much for taking time to appreciate the finer things in life.

As I was telling you, after Momma heard the reading of the will, Hannah came by and they talked about how to progress with the deposition of the unit. They decided it would be the perfect place for Hannah and Patrick to live. Hannah said they were eager to start a family and having a sister close would be perfect family connection. So, as I said earlier, it was decided the loft be deeded to Hannah.

Within the next few days Patrick drew plans for remodeling the three-bedroom portion of the unit into two bedrooms with one master bath, a small nursery, a large walk-in closet and a private bath for the second bedroom. Buddy and I trained our ears to understand him as he explained this to the carpenters.

As they talked and walked through the unit, Buddy and I made our final investigation of the hall and bathroom. The police had released the unit the week before. Although the body was gone, we made a surprising find.

Under a bloody towel, against a side wall between the stool and the bathtub Buddy found three poker chips We knew they didn't belong there, so Buddy carried then home in this mouth and hid them in his bed. I discovered a familiar musty, woody smell on a torn oily rag and carried it home with me. I knew the smell from someplace and thought best not to leave it as the police had not seen fit to take it. I didn't think their smeller was as good as mine.

Everyone had a great time at the party. Princess Daisy had a lovely pink tutu and was the talk of the party. Even Miss Olivia managed to behave, well, as best as possible for her. Buddy and I, well, we ate like kings.

The next Monday after the Halloween Party the construction crews began tearing out walls, electricians assembled their tools, and painters ascended ladders. We watched but stayed out of their way after Buddy knocked over a bucket of pink paint. Neither Jake nor Buddy were happy when the bathtub was used to scrub him pink-less. I can tell you, pink was not Buddy's color, though Miss Daisy looked quite smart in pink.

Chapter 5

Many times, during the seven years we've lived in the warehouse, Miss Daisy had stayed with us when Mr. Cohen went out of town. Let me tell you, she was a fun playmate but quite a handful.

First, she never, and I mean never, ate her food in the bowl it was served in. Bite by bite she removed food from the bowl and walked to a rug in the kitchen where she dropped it, studied it diligently, then delicately downed it. If no rug was there, she walked to the front door mat and dropped it there. Needless to say, it took Daisy a long time to eat her supper. Izzie used to say Daisy's food was digested by the time it hit her tummy.

Miss Daisy came to live with us in early Fall as though it was one of her regular visits. As the days, then weeks, passed there was a chill in the air, and she realized something was wrong. My heart pained when I noticed her eyes had lost their sparkle. She meandered through the loft whining. When I, in sympathy, let her sleep next to me, she was quiet and content. She discovered my Teddy and carried him around like a rag doll. By the way she licked him, I knew she missed her toys. I wasn't given to loaning out my Teddy, still he comforted her, so I said nothing. When she realized Mr. Cohen was never coming back, she stopped brooding and began to enjoy our company. We were lucky we lived across from each other for so many years. Daisy was in a familiar place.

My sweet Momma and I, Jake and Buddy, and Mr. Cohen and Daisy lived on the fourth floor of the four-story warehouse. This was the warehouse Izzie's father bought and renovated into upscale apartments and lofts years before he was murdered by his brother, Jessie. Sometimes Momma talked to Mr. Cohen about her Daddy. I could tell he was fond of Izzie as we listened to stories he told of her Daddy's youth in the boot-hills of Missouri.

Mr. Cohen stayed in contact with Izzie's daddy through the years and moved into his loft soon after her daddy transformed the building into eight units. The Applegates, Harry and Leona, and Miss Gracie Lou Higgenbotham lived on the first floor in Units 1-A and 1-B. Both were original renters. The second and third floor units were also renters.

Of the two fourth floor lofts, one was purchased by Mr. Cohen. The other loft was kept by Matt DeLisle for his family when in the city. The Applegates, I've heard Izzie say when we'd go visit, managed the warehouse and rental apartments since it opened. They handled maintenance and rented a unit whenever one became empty.

Many times, I visited the Applegates on Mah Jongg day. There were four ladies who'd meet every few weeks at Miss Leona's for their Mah Jongg fix and lunch. Olivia, Judy, and Miss Gracie Lou were addicted to the game. I nearly became a professional at this game because I'm a good listener.

"One Bam Bird, two crack, nine dot." Those ladies had their own unusual language which took me several visits to understand. They laughed as they followed their printed cards searching for a winning hand to play. Occasionally, I'd hear one of them yell 'Mah Jongg" and the others around the table would hand her money.

This made no sense to me. Whatever, they didn't understand dog-speak and I didn't understand them.

While they played their weird game, I licked my Dalmatian stuffed dog or snuggled up to Mr. Harry in his easy chair. Sometimes we both snored. The Applegates let me stay with them a lot when Izzie worked a double shift at Saint Jude's which happened every week or so. This was usually the same time Olivia and her friends played their Mah Jongg game. I sometimes wondered if Izzie chose that same day to work in order to dodge her mother's insistence she join the game.

I'd spent many hours listening to the click, click of the tiles as the ladies washed the tiles. I was surprised to learn it wasn't with water.

I eavesdropped one day to hear Miss Leona say, "Okay, ladies, each player's hands must move the tiles around before we make the two rows of nineteen in front of our racks"

Washing the tiles, I came to understand, is the act of stirring the tiles around on the card table.

Arthritis had begun to set in my back legs. I felt like more hours of sleep were needed, I realized there was a lot I didn't know when I was a pup. Especially about human action. I always thought clothes, dishes, humans, and dogs were washed with water and soap. Those Mah Jongg ladies knew a thing or two about cleanliness because they could clean those tiles by merely touching them with their hands.

Their behavior seemed bizarre to me, but I can tell you, those ladies were very serious about their playing. The fourth member, Judy, won most of the games. I heard her say she never spent her winnings and had a drawer full of quarters, dimes and nickels. I think she kind of hid her winnings like I hid my extra bones. Wish I had a drawer to keep mine in. I usually hid mine behind the green tufted cushion on Sweet Momma's lounge chair.

Izzie bought the lounge chair when we moved here. Our loft was never rented but kept for use by the DeLisle family. Before we moved in, Olivia used it when she and her Mah Jongg ladies came to Memphis for shopping and a few fun nights on the town. Maybe those nights lost their appeal. She stopped coming here years ago. The loft had been locked for several years when Izzie and I moved in. We immediately loved it there. The night view of dancing lights on the barges coasting down the Mississippi always made me happy. When I looked out the glass wall to the boats on the river below my tail did a lot of wagging. It made its happy sound. Tap, Tap, Tap.

Several months before, I heard Izzie tell Jake that Mr. Cohen gambled for a living. As a young man, before casinos were in built in Caruthersville, he'd gambled at the cock fights run by her daddy Matt's, brother, Jessie. Their families were old-time friends from way back.

The two fourth floor lofts we had shared with the now deceased opened into a large hall area with brick walls. I looked forward to having Hannah and Patrick as our new neighbors. The hall was where we went to ride in the little room that went up and down. When Momma or anyone pushed a magical button on the wall it opened its doors. Our favorite word GO was often associated with the ride down. Buddy and I would shuffle our bottoms in anticipation of the doors opening. Momma said we did the hula, whatever that was I didn't know. Izzie called the room that moved an elevator, I suppose because it could elevate us whenever she pushed the magic button.

Chapter 6

I zzie and I were home, a month ago, on the night of the murder. We were not alone. Jake and Little Daisy were with us. She'd been staying with us while Mr. Cohen said he was on a business trip. As far as we knew, he was still in Florida. He told Izzie he was going to Ft. Lauderdale. Jake, Izzie's main squeeze, had come up from Nesbit, Mississippi with my pal, Buddy. Izzie and Jake snuggled on the taupe sectional, watched *Friends* and *ER*. Momma muttered about how the TV show was not like her experience at the emergency room at St Jude's, but she laughed at *Friends* and stayed glued to the screen. Izzie's head rested on Jake's strong shoulder. I felt good when I watched them snuggle.

They ate popcorn and drank beer while we three dogs romped around the living room having a good playtime. Buddy had the advantage by size of grabbing the yellow and green squeeze ball. Then, he lay on it. I soon realized not to count Miss Daisy out of the game. She was a cunning little thing. When Buddy hid the ball under his tummy she would bring one of her treat bones, drop it in front of Buddy, just far enough that he would have to stand up to reach it. Then, when he stood to get it, Daisy or I snatched the ball. A grand game. We played this over and over for hours until Daisy ran out of the treats she'd hidden in my bed.

None of us heard anything during our play time the evening of Mr. Cohen's killing. Nothing which sounded like a pop, pop. Perhaps it is because all the interior walls are brick, except the glass wall which looks out on the Mississippi.

We woke the next morning to a grey fall drizzle. A fog-like mist lay over the Mississippi as I looked below. We finished our downward dog stretches just as Jake grabbed his jacket and our leashes from the hall tree. Once he put on his jacket we knew he would take the three of us to the courtyard for our morning nature call.

"Are you taking them for a walk as well? Looks like this drizzle could produce a storm at any minute."

"No walk," answered Jake. "Just their morning call."

Izzie said, "I'll run over to Mr. Cohen's loft and water the plants as soon as I load our breakfast dishes. See you in a bit."

We finished our morning outing. The heavy drizzle required all of us to be towel dried. Jake accomplished the task, easily with me and Daisy, not so easy with Buddy who squirmed and shook off the towel. Then Buddy snatched the towel from Jake and ran through the loft. Jake laughed when he finally caught him. Sometimes they acted like kids. Finished, we headed to the TV room to play ball. It was then we heard Izzie scream. Her yell made my ears come erect, my skin prickle.

She burst through the front door, slipped on the door mat and fell into Jake's arms as he ran to greet her. She trembled, had difficulty getting out the words, "Mr. Cohen, he's," she continued to scream, her face white like snow that would blanket our world come December, "dead. Mr. Cohen's dead."

"Sweetheart calm down. What are you screaming about?"

Izzie stammered, "He's dead, he's been murdered, call the police."

"What in the world are you talking about? Who's dead?"

"Mr. Cohen. Blood's everywhere. Why was he home? I thought he was in Florida."

The confusion of the moment provided the perfect time for me to investigate the situation that caused Momma's distress. I quietly sneaked across the hall. Man, I couldn't believe my eyes. What was always a meticulous placement of chairs, tables, and lamps was in unbelievable chaos. Furniture turned over, broken and smashed. A red color trailed from the living room, down the hall and into the bathroom. As I trotted down the hallway I picked up on something that made my hair bristle. Then, I got a good whiff. On the spot, I knew it was blood. Mr. Cohen's blood.

Wow, what a mess. The condition of Mr. Cohen's body was far beyond anything I had seen on those Mr. Perry Mason shows. Blood spatters covered the walls, floor, and Mr. Cohen. Blood dripped from fingers of one arm flung over the side of the tub. His blood-soaked shirt was torn and ripped. Glassy eyes stared upward toward someone or something that wasn't there. Odd, I thought. Why was a blood-soaked rag and a poker chip falling from his mouth?

An odor I could not place instantly terrified me. I recoiled at the smell, my heart did that thumping it does when I'm on alert. It was a musty, woody, leathery smell from the past. I couldn't put my nose to it, not sure what I remembered, but I wanted out of there. Fast.

My tummy was queasy. I thought I would lose it. I ran back to our loft as fast as my short legs would carry me. Buddy wanted to hear about what I'd seen. We dog-spoke quietly and spared little Daisy who was curled in a circle, asleep in my bed. After Izzie called the police she told Jake she was glad she'd left Daisy playing with me and Buddy. Daisy did not need to witness the bloody scene nor see her loving life-time companion as Izzie, and I, found him.

It was sometime later when Buddy and I sneaked over, under the yellow tape, for him to investigate everything I'd seen.

Chapter 7

On the day Momma found Mr. Cohen, policemen in navy blue uniforms arrived like ants on a ham bone. They were everywhere. Izzie answered their unrelenting questions while other officers examined every inch of Mr. Cohen's apartment.

Five days went by before Momma could retrieve Princess Daisy's toys, bed, pink jacket and yellow raincoat. Daisy was glad to have her bed, but I only laid in it one time. It crinkled and seemed lumpy to me. Not having all her toys, Daisy had tried to latch on to my green turtle, but I set her straight on that action. She settled on Teddy which I had accepted for the time. Now she had her favorites and could leave mine alone.

Funny, Buddy never took any of my toys, except the yellow and green striped ball. Daisy had become my sister-dog, laid against my back to stay calm, but she did irritate me half to death with her finicky habits. Buddy was always the same, dependable in a crisis, unselfish with all his toys and never took my prize turtle. He would always be my best-ever dog friend. We were pals.

We began to settle into a new routine when, a week after the murder, two men dressed in identically tailored suits, one charcoal grey and one midnight blue, knocked on our door. The black forest cuckoo clock on the kitchen wall chirped a two-note song when Jake, who with Buddy was in the living room, answered the it. Buddy did his low growl until Jake tugged on his collar meaning to be quiet.

The men showed Jake their shiny metal badges and introduced themselves as Special Agents of the Internal Revenue Service Criminal Investigation Division. They revealed they had been conducting an investigation into alleged violations of the IRS code regarding Mr. Cohen prior to his death. They indicated that due to his alleged murder, other law enforcement agencies would be involved in the weeks to come.

Without invitation Mr. Grey Suit walked in and sat on the taupe sectional facing the glass wall windows. Mr. Blue Suit followed close behind and also took a seat on the sectional. With a stern expression and a voice like my squeaky turtle, Grey Suit said they wanted to clarify some information from Izzie's earlier conversations with the local police. Izzie, who was in the kitchen, listened in amazement as she put the final heaping scoop of sugar in the pitcher of iced tea she'd just brewed.

Blue Suit had nothing to say as he glanced around the living room. He was pleasant enough, didn't mind when I jumped on the sectional beside him. He scratched behind my right ear in that hard to reach place and then asked Izzie questions about who rode the elevator and who used the fire exit.

I forgot to mention there was a fire escape at the end of the hall with a red exit sign over it. Never in all my years did we use that exit. I explored the metal landing one day when the window cleaners were here, I'm sure my small paws would have had trouble balancing on those metal steps, if I tried to go down them.

Grey Suit snorted as he drew in a breath and took charge of the questioning. I heard the words Black Russian. Not knowing any Russians, I let it pass. Not wise, I learned later. Another interesting question was asked. The short man, Grey Suit, inquired if the family ever derived any closure from the Jessie DeLisle incident? His line of questioning appeared unnecessary to me when they came to talk about Mr. Cohen.

After the explosion of Izzie's boat, two years ago, the family assumed Uncle Jessie died in the explosion despite no corpse ever being retrieved. I remember hearing Izzie tell Hannah the coroner said it was not unusual in such an incidence as an explosion, especially one that took place in the water.

Two years ago, on that summer day, Izzie and I were alone with Uncle Jessie on her cruiser in the Mississippi River. He drank heavily as she told him she had the letter Clarabelle had written proving he killed her Father. We believed Jessie tried to kill us when Izzie accused him of committing that murder. He referred to some information he had and said he was compelled to do it to free her Mother, Olivia, from their Father's outbursts of rage. He shocked us when he made reference to killing Clarabelle, Patrick's grandmother.

Everything he confessed to Izzie was radio transmitted through the boat's radio back to shore for the police to record. Momma and I were frightened he might hurt us because he wanted the letter Clarabelle had written against him. Izzie didn't have the letter on the cruiser. It was safely hidden at her apartment. Unknown to Jessie, we jumped off the boat into the river and swam toward shore. The blast caused waves so strong, they nearly drowned us. Everyone thought Jessie died in the blast. Was there more to his death? Buddy and I needed to cogitate about these questions as soon as those unwanted guests left.

Buddy and I love to watch Perry Mason. We learned a lot about how detectives should follow clues to solve crimes. Izzie calls it our TV School of Investigation. This happens when she goes to work or when Buddy and I are not invited to GO, a grave and disappointing experience for us.

We were keen on the word GO and would stop all forms of play when we heard that word. I will admit, in the fall watching Perry Mason was our third-best activity next to GO and ball snatching. In summer our second-best activity was jumping in Jake's pool on the ranch in Nesbit, Mississippi. Our drive to the ranch was usually a thirty-minute drive from Memphis, though I've been riding shotgun when Izzie's driven it in twenty minutes. I've been known to conceive some serious prayers on those trips with Momma. I always needed playtime to relax when we got to Nesbit.

Grey Suit sucked in some air and snorted again as he spoke. I focused and cocked my head right to hear every word of his questioning with my good ear. His nasal voice began to irritate me. I searched around the loft and found Buddy and Daisy curled up in their beds behind the back side of the sectional. I ambled over, lay in my bed to rest my eyes a bit and continued to listen to the conversation of the two men in suits.

Maybe I dozed for just a minute. I was awakened by the crash of a glass on the coffee table. While serving the suits, my adorable klutzy, Izzie, dropped a glass of iced tea. The glass hit the limestone tabletop which showed no mercy. Iced cubes and tea splashed over Agent Grey Suit.

There was a scurry of activity as most of the glass and tea were wiped up. The agents abruptly stood to leave. Grey Suit scowled as he continued to wipe tea from his suit jacket with a wet, soggy paper towel. With his irritating pitched voice, he took a deep breath, snorted and declared the case was far from closed. He vowed to return for further questioning.

Jake saw them to the door. Izzie fell onto the sectional and picked up her glass of sweet tea. Jake poured himself something stronger from the bottle marked XXX Reserve on the label.

"I'll not let this rest," Izzie voice was angry and defiant. "If they think I'm waiting around for them to find Uncle Jessie, they sure are wrong. He's damaged this family enough when we learned he was Hannah's real father and killed our father and Patrick's grandmother. Enough of him, I say."

Jake answered, "Let's share the theory he is still alive with Patrick and Hannah. Get their take on this new information and set a plan."

Buddy rose from his comfy bed, did his shoulder stretch and gave me a nudge with his wet nose. It was time Buddy and I did our cogitating about the days curious happenings. What a morning we'd experienced. Both of us were in a bit of a daze.

With the agents gone, Izzie and Jake finished their drinks, then began hanging cobwebs and streamers for the Masquerade Halloween Party.

Chapter 8

Mr. Cuckoo left his house and chirped twelve notes for us just as Hannah and Patrick strode through the front door with sacks of mouth-watering smells. Saliva dripped from each side of Buddy's mouth. They'd brought Big Al's barbeque. Thankfully, there was enough for our lunch and the Halloween party that evening.

I was reminded of the traditional dog daze of summer barbeque mother Olivia used to throw every Fourth of July. Good food, good friends, good music and unfortunately, what I hated—fireworks. Everything was great except the blasting ear-piercing fireworks. Buddy and I always hid with our paws over our ears to block out some of the sound.

Speaking of sound. I knew he was a wicked uncle, but I missed hearing the music of Uncle Jessie's band. Everyone enjoyed his velvety, smooth voice. He had a flair the audience loved. Jessie would pull up to the grandstand on his black Harley, rev up the motor like a professional driver, guitar over his shoulder, then jump onto the stage to immense applause from his fans.

Olivia's July parties are now over. She never mentioned having another after the incident of the cruiser explosion. Each year since, in October, Izzie hosted a masked Halloween Party which was lots of fun and, I'm thankful to report, without any fireworks.

Izzie's masked Halloween party provided me with one problem. I could only be sure of knowing the dogs. Every human wore a mask which forced me to put my sniffer to work to identify them. It was essential to make the identification to know which guest to approach for a treat. The experience was easy for a super sleuth like me and loads of fun. Buddy and Daisy were of no help until the treats were handed out. Daisy would sit up and beg, sometimes stealing my paw-shaking act. Buddy could get a treat by staring directly at a guest, perhaps laying his chocolate head on their lap and giving them his sad puppy dog eyes.

Some of the gals wore the same perfume and the same goes for the guys so it was difficult to tell them apart. I could usually identify the ones who sweat a lot. Man, I could get a whiff and I knew for certain their name even if they were dressed in some silly, crazy outfit. Naturally I knew my immediate family, but last year I didn't guess Miss Leona and Harry who came as Raggedy Ann and Andy. They smelled like gingerbread. Guests can get real creative with their outfits in order to win Izzie's prize of a six-course dinner at The Peabody, Memphis' downtown hotel known for local history and scrumptious food.

Momma and Hannah took me to the Peabody back when my bladder was easy to control. I'm sorry to admit, my barking was not in control. I was a puppy being socialized. We were instantly told by a man in a police-type uniform to leave the main lobby. I never understood why it was wrong to bark at those ducks as they waddled off the elevator toward the water fountain. At Olivia's ranch I barked at the little creatures and they just honked back. To this day, I think those Peabody ducks must be spoiled. They were not very friendly.

For the masked party Momma and Jake dressed as a French Maid and

Butler. She said those costumes helped hostesses move around easily, chatter with guests and pick out the costume winners. I thought they looked smart and sassy but for sure would not give a prize to themselves. Patrick and Hannah were dressed as Count Dracula and a beautiful Bride of Dracula. They held hands and once they kissed as they bobbed for apples. The bobbing activity seemed silly to me. We canines learned early in our puppy years to just accept the odd things our humans do.

I wondered what costume Olivia would wear. We knew she was bringing a guest. I thought he might be someone from the Memphis Yacht Club. She goes there a lot. I've heard her tell Izzie she was on her way to the club many times at the end of our visits. Izzie told Jake neither she nor Hannah had met Olivia's date for the party. Don't guess it mattered since I wouldn't see his face.

Maybe I'd know him from his yacht club smell or maybe his voice. I'm good at smells and voices too. My sweet Momma let Buddy, Daisy, and me lay under the table when they ate outside on the yacht club patio. After listening to people's conversations, Buddy and I would peek out to see who was talking. We soon learned to identify people by their voices. Daisy showed no interest in my voice game and preferred to watch for tidbits handed to her. It was at the club I also learned about steak, raw if you please, and asparagus, two of my favorite foods in the whole world.

Speaking of favorite foods, Momma served something she called dragon toes. To me it was the usual grilled asparagus wrapped in bacon. Daisy turned her nose up but, ok, with me. I got her serving. She did take a deviled egg to the kitchen rug and delicately ate the yellow yoke as it crumbled on Momma's rug. It took time, but eventually she ate every crumb.

Once, shortly after Daisy moved in with our family, I growled at the Princess when she put food on a rug. I'd never been permitted to do such things and thought I'd set her straight on how we do things in this family. Can you believe this? My Izzie told me to stop my growl because Daisy was old and an heiress. I still didn't know what being old has to do with bad manners. I talked to Buddy and he said he thought like I did. He woofed 'the money was the deciding factor', then moseyed off to his bed for a nap. So much for being the poor member of this household.

Chapter 9

Compared to the heiress, Buddy, Sabbath and I were probably poor. But, we had loving parents, like Mr. and Mrs. Shin-Lee from 2-B, who treated Sabbath, their red Doberman, like a son. We enjoyed good food and lots of play time, so we didn't mind at all. In fact, we didn't notice. We gobbled our party food from our bowls while the Princess carried every morsel to the kitchen rug. For a big Doberman, Sabbath was a very neat eater and drank his water like Olivia sips her merlot, easy. Buddy, on the other hand, had not changed in all the years I'd known him. He splashed his water over the floor creating an invitation for Izzie to do one of her swan dances.

That's the name I call her as she flops her arms and tries to balance herself. Jake says she's a lovely klutz. I probably shouldn't tell you. I never like to tell bad things about my Momma, but my Izzie really is a klutz. Water is just one of the things that can cause her to slide and sometimes fall. It's not her fault. She likes to wear white tennis shoes with her jeans and often she forgets to tie the shoelaces. Those shoelaces are usually the cause, that is, unless she trips over my Teddy. She is fairly adept at catching herself, so she seldom has to put her nursing skills to use.

Instead of butler and French maid costumes, Jake and Momma could've dressed like a nurse and doctor. I guess everyone, especially her nursing buddies from St. Jude's, would have guessed who they were. I knew some of the guests were her nurse friends from the whiff of lavender soap. I could not forget them. They were the gals from the late-night nurse parties I remembered Izzie used to have on the cruiser.

The four couples from downstairs floors, two and three, were easy to figure out, especially when Sabbath kept laying down beside the Asian couple from 2-B. Sabbath was a handsome red Doberman with muscled forelegs. An erect head and shoulders added to his majestic fierce look. He was not at all fierce unless someone, like Daisy, took his raw-hide bone or if someone touched Mrs. Shin-Lee. Sabbath would snarl and show his teeth in a way that convinced even me not to upset him.

The other couples from floors two and three were easy to identify by their laughter. Miss Gracie Lou Higgenbotham from 1-B, across from Harry and Leona, was always a real hoot at a party. With a big, red plastic nose and giant feet, she looked comical in her red and white polka-dot clown outfit. She laughed a lot as the evening wore on and tried her best to juggle three red balls without much success. When she dropped them Buddy would grab one, then Jake would chase him to get it back. Miss Gracie Lou was a good sport about the balls and although in her eighties, she drank Izzie's spiked cranberry punch like a thirsty sailor.

Not that I've known any thirsty sailors, but Perry Mason compared drinking to one on his latest show, so it must be so. Perry Mason and Izzie were the two people I believe to always be truthful and set me straight. I usually turned my head sideways with my good right ear to hear every word because I didn't want to miss anything they said. One time, Momma's words caused me concern. I heard her say Mr. Mason was dead. It's not like me to say my Momma is wrong but I knew this time she was terribly wrong. The day before I'd seen him on his morning television show.

The night of the big party, the loft was lit in semi-darkness. Shadows on the walls created a foreboding atmosphere. My leg muscles twitched as we rambled from room to room. Was something bad surrounding us? My heart pounded. I had an overpowering sense of dread as Daisy, Sabbath, and I wandered about looking for treats. Daisy shook off her tiara but still wore her tutu. A scarf around our necks was all Buddy and I tolerated.

Music howled like wolves in the winter. This did nothing to ease my fears as the evening wore on. Candles and skeletons hanging in the doorways increased my eerie feeling. I looked around for Buddy. Daisy and I didn't know where he had gone. He was nowhere to be seen. Why did he leave us when we might need him? I was certain without Buddy, Sabbath would protect us. As Daisy and I ventured into the hallway I noticed to the right side the elevator was a round table. Heavy cobwebs hung all around. Before the party goers arrived, I remembered hearing Jake say something to Izzie as he carried a cardboard box to the hall and set it on the table.

"I'll put the dry ice in the pumpkin. The pumpkin is large enough for you to set your punch bowl inside. It should balance on the dry ice and stay cold all evening."

Izzie placed a big bowl of red liquid inside the pumpkin. "There's enough rum in this bowl to add punch until sun-up," Izzie laughed.

Daisy, Sabbath, and I stood in the hall watching the party goers laugh and talk. We were about to get a meatball treat from Miss Leona when I glanced across the hall and noticed smoke coming from the punch table. I assumed the hall was going up in flames and barked to alarm everyone. I barked at the top of my masculine voice. Sabbath and Daisy chimed in. We three sounded the alarm.

Buddy was not there, maybe he was scared and hiding or still asleep. Everyone came running from the loft into the hall, but no one made an attempt to escape. I continued to bark. To my amazement, suddenly everyone applauded. Izzie must have thought me funny. She laughed as she bent down, picked me up and gave me a big hug and announced I was her protector as well as her Love Sponge.

Even though she said the dry ice caused the problem, I had been quite alarmed and continued to growl under my breath. Daisy stopped abruptly. Sabbath only quieted down after several minutes. Understand, I'd now had time to ponder the confusing incident and concluded humans are difficult to understand. We later found Buddy snoring in his favorite spot behind the sectional, his head resting on his paws. Partly hidden between his paws lay the poker chips he'd found earlier. Perhaps he'd fallen asleep pondering a thought, luckily, he was oblivious to my embarrassing incident.

My problem with the not-a-fire incident was I faced another one of those human sayings that did not make sense. Ice is like cold water, wet. Dry is like dirt, dry. How can humans talk about dry ice? Their actions puzzled a clear thinker like me. It was baffling. I thought I was wise to warn everyone no matter what my sweet Izzie said. Well, I tried.

We three scampered back into the loft to find some guests gathered around the Ouija board. Others were trying the levitation game. When someone said she bet dogs could play "Light as a Feather, Stiff as a Board", I got out of her way in a hurry and went to find Buddy. Body floating business was too creepy for me.

Talk about floating. At that precise moment, in walked, I should say, in floated Olivia. Although wearing a white mask of a beautiful lady I knew it was her by the faint fragrance of gardenia that surrounded her. She was lovely in a long dress of lavender and pink. The fabric was thin, like a cloud or puffs of mist that settled over the Mississippi. Her escort was a tall man with a mask black on one side and white on the other. They were a party-stopping pair. In true classic Olivia style, they caught everyone's attention as they stepped out of the elevator.

Her escort was charming as he bowed and kissed many of the ladies' hands. While Mr. Handsome was courting the ladies, I sniffed my way through the party goers to follow the scent of lavender. It led me to the open bar in the kitchen. Oh my, could Olivia be starting on the hard stuff so soon? Much to my surprise she filled a glass with tonic water, added a lime slice and turned to approach the other guests.

I stood on the kitchen floor, head slightly turned to study her. Shocked at what happened next, I didn't know how to react.

Olivia reached down, smiling, and scratched the hard-to-reach spot behind my right ear. Then she put a finger straight-up over her lips. I knew this was a human way of saying, "don't tell". Who did she think I'd tell? Who would care that she wasn't boozing it up tonight? There were no dog-speakers around. This from a woman who, in the past, screamed at me to get away from her closet. I had no explanation for the change in her behavior.

Unless, the reason Olivia was nice to me was because she was happy. She certainly wasn't acting mad at anyone. She was, I was shocked to think, even pleasant. Maybe her gentleman friend gave her a reason to be cheerful. She began to work the room. Her face, hidden by the mask, approached each guest with a laugh that was friendly and a bit flirtatious. She was the alluring Olivia, an example of southern charm and grace.

Hannah pulled Izzie aside. "Did you notice Mother? She's really enjoying this and being cheerful to everyone."

"Yes, I caught that. I expected she'd only talk to Miss Gracie Lou and Leona, her Mah Jongg buddies. She's all over the house, greeting everyone. What about her guest?"

"Captivating and pleasant. Perhaps handsome. I can't wait until everyone removes their masks." Izzie answered.

"We'll find out soon. Jake's ready to announce the costume winners and I think they are the front-runners. Here he comes with the pumpkin trophies."

Jake yelled. No one could hear him. Someone finally turned down the music. "Gather around everyone. You all really went all out with your costumes. We wish there were fifteen gifts but, hell, we couldn't afford that many prizes for the Peabody. Since we are not at the opera, we would like to congratulate the winners who looked like they were from the cast of The Phantom of the Opera. Will the lady with the white mask and her partner with the Phantom mask step forward?"

Everyone clapped and waited. No one came forward. They clapped again and waited. The couple had disappeared.

Chapter 10

The cuckoo bird left his clock house on the kitchen wall and sang three notes as the unmasked guests grabbed their coats and said their good-byes.

Izzie and Jake stood by the elevator. Izzie uttered a sigh of relief as she leaned her head on Jake's shoulder.

"It's late." She said, "Can you believe it? Let's clean this hallway and turn in."

"I agree. We've thrown quite a party." Jake kissed her forehead. "For once, all I can think about is sleep," he said.

It was hard to miss the gleam in his drooping eyes.

Arthritis in my right hip was giving me discomfort from the running back and forth picking up treats from the guests. It was time for bed. Daisy snuggled next to me as we collapsed in my bed from the events of the evening. Her snuggling became more frequent, especially when she was really tired. I slept soundly, consumed by my ongoing dream of chasing the uninvited mouse into the kitchen pantry.

The sun was starting to show on the horizon when I was abruptly awakened by Buddy's bark. He woofed, waking everyone telling us he needed to answer nature's call. I needed to finish my dream. Buddy's needs won.

We canines did our downward dog stretches and rolled around on our backs before Jake appeared from the bedroom in crumpled pajamas and bushy hair. Izzie was nowhere to be seen. Jake grabbed a raincoat, opened the front door, stumbled across the hall and pressed the magic button for us. As we bolted inside Buddy whimpered, he might not make it to the courtyard. He didn't.

The ride back up to the loft was uneventful. All was calm until Jake began cleaning the elevator floor. He was on his hands and knees when someone below must have pushed the button because the doors closed and down he went. We heard him yell some of those words Momma calls bad words.

Sweet Momma and Jake discussed the reason for Olivia's disappearance as they collected dirty glasses and plates. Jake tackled the task of vacuuming while Izzie loaded the dishwasher.

Around noon, the loft appeared normal and my pals and I got a two-block walk. The sun broke through the rain clouds of earlier making it a great day for our play time. Glad to be outside, we let off some steam. The three of us rolled and sprinted through the fallen leaves, many of which stuck to mine and Daisy's fur. Buddy tried to catch the unfriendly squirrel, then we chased after the ball Jake threw as we raced along Riverside Drive.

The rest of the day was spent with a few final touches of packing away the decorations and arranging the loft back into an orderly interior. When humans say they are going to "throw" a party they should consider all the stuff that is thrown by their guests. To be sure, this group of happy friends were a messy bunch. Jake even had to clean cranberry juice from the bedroom carpet. Why, pray tell, was someone drinking cranberry punch in the bedroom?

We finished our evening meal of kibble, liver, and sweet potato. I ambled over to the glass wall, my favorite spot in the loft. Favorite, except, of course, for Izzie's bed. I liked to get comfy once I snuggle into the bend of her legs. As I mentioned before, this sleeping pattern happened when we shared our special, just us, nights together.

Now don't get me wrong. I liked Jake. He was one of my most favorite people, but in bed he always got closer to Izzie than me and this cramped my style. He'd be so close to her I couldn't wedge between them. So, when he was at the loft I usually gave up, let them have their privacy and slept in my own bed.

The sun was sinking into the Mississippi as I stared out the glass wall looking toward the river. My eyes blinked, the way they do before I get into my dream about the pantry mouse. Gusts of air howled around the brick corner of the building. Whitecaps blew on the Mississippi below. An eerie wind moaned as my eyes drooped. What could possible happen next? A loud beating at the front door snapped me out of my daydream and answered my question.

Izzie opened the door to find Miss Leona waving her hands and muttering something about a smoke smell in her apartment. She'd checked with 2A and 3A and found no problem. Could the smell be coming from Mr. Cohen's vacant unit? Her unit was on his side of the warehouse, three floors down. She couldn't find her extra key. She said she may have given both keys to the construction crew superintendent when the remodeling started.

Izzie snatched her keys from the hall table and darted across the hall. Leona followed close behind. Jake ran behind them with the fire-extinguisher. They rushed across the hall, unlocked the door and discovered the back area of the Cohen loft filled with smoke. My black nose burned from the fumes. Someone or something put my Izzie, all of us, in danger. Lucky for us, Leona, like me, had a good smeller.

Patrick and Hannah came early the next morning, surveyed the mess and agreed with the contractor it would now be the end of November before they could move in. Hannah's face was pale. Perhaps tired from the party the night before. I took care to watch her in case my help was needed. Her face was puffy too, maybe my imagination. Too much cranberry punch? Maybe gaining weight?

Hannah and Patrick's soon-to-be home was a mess of smelly carpet and grey discolored walls. The few boxes they'd brought from Nashville were not damaged. Even the woodwork was streaked. She called it constructive chaos.

Now there was smoke damage to contend with in addition to a murder to solve.

Chapter 11

A few weeks later Izzie and Hannah attended a service at the Happy Valley Funeral Home. Several residents from our building attended Mr. Cohen's memorial service along, of course, with Daisy and me. Hannah was there in case Izzie couldn't handle Daisy, which was no problem since I was in charge.

As mourners were being seated, I noticed, sitting in the back row, six men I'd never seen before.

A portly gentleman sat next to the aisle. His round head was completely bald although his chubby face was pleasant enough. To his left a stern-faced man sported a red-tinted beard as he stared straight ahead. To his left, a head taller than the rest, sat a cowboy, defined by his western cut clothes. Continuing to his left sat a dapper elderly man wearing a dark suit, white shirt, and tie. To his left was a shorter man in all black wearing tortoise framed glasses and a black suede skull-cap kippah on his head. Finally, I spied a man whose grim expression I found objectionable. He was unable to sit still, held his head kind of sideways or maybe he was somehow out of balance.

On the opposite side of the aisle and two pews in front of this group sat the lawyer I'd met at the reading of the will. He occasionally glanced sideways to the men across the aisle. Perhaps he knew them.

I knew this was not a traditional Jewish service because we were in a funeral home. His service should, as is Jewish custom, have been the day after he died except his corpse was being examined for clues to establish cause of death. No Rabbi was present, so the man with the skullcap read something I think was in Hebrew.

Harry and Leona Applegate, the apartments managers from 1-A, completed the group of attendees, none shedding any tears. Mr. Cohen was liked, not loved.

The service was nothing like the funeral mass two years ago for Clarabelle, Izzie's nanny and Patrick's grandmother. Her service lasted over an hour with a lot of crying, especially at the hole dropping ceremony behind the church. Today's service was short and to the point. A few words from the undertaker and we were out of there. Did Daisy realize we were paying tribute to a man who loved her so much he left everything he owned for her care. Probably not.

I didn't feel the sadness I felt at Patrick's grandmother's funeral. Maybe because it was a mass, maybe because Clarabelle had been like a mother to Izzie and Hannah. All the family suspected she was suffocated by Uncle Jessie because she had information linking him to the crime. She had written her recollections of the crime and hid the letter in her ironing board. Izzie discovered the letter when she was turning it into a table. Two years and I still missed our walks on the Nesbit ranch.

I did experience a more exciting day after the Mr. Cohen's service. Hannah drove when we left the Happy Valley Funeral Home. Instead of going straight home she crept through noon traffic, pulling into a parking lot beside a big tall building. She abruptly stopped the car and told Izzie they were going inside to get test results. The sisters chattered and giggled in the front seat.

Then they bounced out of the car. Hannah leaned her head inside,

"Sammy, it's a cool day so we're leaving you and Daisy in the car while Izzie and I go inside. Thirty minutes, at the most, and we'll be back."

Izzie should have told her sister, we dogs don't wear watches. I cannot tell time unless I count the cuckoos. I let it ride. The gals hoofed it toward the big double doors. I was still pondering some deep thought about why we were here when suddenly they were back. Laughing and talking a mile a minute, Hannah inched out of the lot and we headed home.

"When will you tell Patrick you're expecting a baby? Tonight?" Izzie asked.

"No, I'll keep the news one more day," Hannah said. "Remember, we're having a party tomorrow evening to celebrate moving into our loft. I'll tell him before the party then we can announce it together. I've invited two couples from work, you and Jake. Don't tell Jake. Everyone will think it's a house-warming party. Man, will Patrick be surprised when he learns there is more good news than finally moving into our new space."

I winked at Daisy to let her know we could tell Buddy about the baby even though Izzie could not tell Jake.

Chapter 12

I admit some memories became foggy during those past few years. My muzzle started to turn grey and my back legs were sometimes stiff from arthritis, but the day of Hannah's announcement is one forever infused in my brain. My heart ached at the thought of it. I recall that day like it happened yesterday.

On the morning of Hannah's planned announcement, Daisy and I answered nature's call. We each got a boiled egg with our morning dog treat. Izzie poured a second cup of coffee, grabbed her phone and we walked across to Hannah's loft. They giggled as they got to work arranging Hannah's apartment

During the day, with the help of the movers from Parker Department Store, they arranged the loft into a cozy, welcoming home. The final furniture delivery brought the pregnant sister her two most cherished items, an upholstered rocker and a wood carved cradle on a stand. Her week's work was finalized. Both gals stood at the nursery doorway, arms around each other's waist, and smiled with approval.

We walked back across the hall to our apartment. Momma went in her bathroom and reappeared sometime later. I could tell by the little ringlets around her face that her auburn hair had been shampooed. Instead of her usual ponytail it hung to her shoulders touching the camel turtleneck she'd tucked into dark brown tailored slacks. A thin brown leather belt and dangling earrings completed her look. I followed her, as the saying goes, like a love-sick puppy, across the hall.

Hannah was in the kitchen arranging plates and glasses on the granite counter. She flitted around like a schoolgirl preparing for her first date. Patrick, she told Izzie, would be home soon.

Aside from Hannah's frequent runs to the bathroom, the sisters were in great shape when the Thai food was delivered at five-thirty. The gals placed the food on a hot tray, set out forks and napkins. All was ready.

Jake and Buddy arrived. Patrick was due any minute. When the guests arrived at six, Hannah served drinks to all but herself, knowing those days of consuming a cold beer with her Thai were over for the next few months.

"It's six-thirty, Hannah. Do you want me to call Patrick to see how late he'll be?" asked Izzie.

"No, He's probably caught in the evening traffic," Hannah said as she ran toward the bathroom.

Izzie gave the guests a tour of the recently redecorated loft. One door, the nursery, remained shut as they began their tour. Through the chatter, I heard a lot of oos and ahs as their friends surveyed the palest of green décor and modern chrome lighting fixtures.

An abrupt knock on the front door startled me. I had an unsettling feeling as I followed Izzie to the door. She opened the door. Two policemen in starched navy uniforms and stern expressions asked for Hannah.

Izzie invited them in and ran down the hall to get her sister. As Hannah approached, the policemen came toward her. The taller of the two began to speak.

"Mrs. Guffin, we are sorry to report there has been an accident involving Professor Patrick Guffin. You are listed as the one to inform in this situation."

Wide-eyed Hannah cried out, "What happened? Is he hurt? Where is he?"

"Madam, would you please step into the hallway so we can speak in private?"

Izzie pulled her sister close as she held her around the waist. The sisters stepped into the hallway. The policeman continued.

"Professor Guffin, we believe, parked his car down the street from Ginger's Florist Shop. Leaving the shop with a bouquet of flowers in hand he walked back toward his car when the accident occurred. As he stepped off the curb, a motorcyclist hit him with such force he was thrown in the path of on-coming traffic.

"Is he alive?" Hannah mumbled.

"Luckily, he was not hit again. Mr. Guffin lay in the street as the motorcyclist fled. Eye-witnesses reported the cycle appeared to be a streamlined black FXRS Harley."

As Hannah slumped forward, Jake rushed to grab her. He eased her onto the leather sofa while Izzie stood frozen in place.

"The ambulance has taken him to the Elvis Presley Trauma Center. Although the accident was serious, he was conscious when taken from the scene. We've had no updates on this condition. You are free to visit him there. This is all we can report at this time." They turned and left as swiftly as they appeared.

Guests sprang into action. Some collected used paper cups and plates, throwing them in the trash as others covered food, storing it in the refrigerator. Jake unplugged the electric serving trays as friends gathered their coats to leave. One of the couples said their good-byes and made a hasty retreat saying they would go to the hospital to console Hannah. Another couple stayed back waiting until they heard from her in case she needed something from the apartment.

I followed Hannah and Izzie into Hannah's bedroom. They put some clothes, a toothbrush, and pill bottles in a small blue case. Jake called me to come as he went across the hall to unlock our unit. Daisy, Buddy, and I ran in. He gave us fresh water, called Miss Leona to come up for our evening feed and walk, grabbed his jacket and was gone.

I took charge to keep Buddy and Daisy calm, and not allow them to mess up the loft. If I could've reached the little magic button in the hallway, we would have been okay. I would gladly have taken charge of going to the courtyard. We always kept hidden treats around the loft, so we never have gone hungry.

True to her dependable nature, Leona appeared as the sun found its resting place behind the mighty Mississippi. She let us answer nature's call in the courtyard. We moseyed to their unit, had a long visit with Mr. Harry and got some yummy treats before heading upstairs. There was nothing more to do, so we slept. I dreamed I came close to catching my mouse as he grabbed a cookie crumb left by one of the guests.

Neither my Momma nor Jake came home until late the next day. Miss Leona took good care of us. While Momma and Jake ate their supper of left-over Thai, they talked about Patrick's condition. Izzie started to load the dishwasher. There was a knock. Hannah appeared, shoulders slumped, her body drooped.

The sun had long disappeared behind the Mississippi when Izzie assisted Hannah across the hall into her loft and back to her bedroom. I followed along in case I was needed to comfort Hannah. She remained there without a sound except for whimpering I heard as I lay outside her door. After Hannah was settled, I followed Momma home.

Two sunsets came and went before Hannah came across the hall to our kitchen for a cup of coffee. She was pale. Her forehead creased from deep frown lines. Her voice rambled as she talked about Patrick's condition.

Hannah was spiraling downward. By the strained whisper of her voice I understood the sadness that gripped her. Feelings of joy derived from the anticipation of becoming a mother were diminished by the fear of what lay ahead. Would her husband live? Would he be crippled for life? Days, maybe years, took a bitter turn for our dear Hannah and Patrick. Celebrations for the birth of their first child had taken second place to the worry and concern over her husband's recovery.

Chapter 13

Preparations for our Thanksgiving celebration began in earnest five days before the big day when Izzie put the turkey in the refrigerator to thaw and cooked cranberries. I heard them pop. Daisy ran into the kitchen wide-eyed. She'd never heard cranberries pop before. It's a scary sound if you've had no experience in the kitchen.

Momma took an English Muffin from the toaster, smeared it with butter and peach colored jam. She made a phone call, turned on the speaker, at the same time as she nibbled her muffin and added sugar to the bubbling berries.

"Mother, were you awake yet? I hope I didn't call too early. It is after seven. I'm just checking the Thanksgiving menu. You're bringing sweet potato pie, right? I'll have a pecan pie and the whipped cream."

"Yes, Izzie, my usual. What time are we eating?"

"Probably one-thirty or whenever Hannah gets back from the hospital. Does your gentleman friend enjoy a drink before his dinner? Leona is bringing some appetizers. Why not come around one o'clock? I'll tell Hannah we'll visit and wait for her."

"Great. Izzie, what have you heard about the investigation of Mr. Cohen's death?' Olivia asked. "Seems all hush, hush. Nothing in the papers. No more questions. What do you suppose is being done to catch his killer?"

"I've heard nothing. Our attention has been directed toward Patrick's welfare more than giving any thought regarding the status of the investigation.

Hannah lived most of those days at the hospital. According to Izzie, she reluctantly accepted the fact Patrick's spinal cord injury could mean complete loss of his legs. Hannah also had the remodeling work to contend with. She possessed no aptitude for directing the workmen whose task was now to modify the loft to be wheelchair ready. To help her, Jake spent as much time as he could spare from management of the ranch to supervise the work.

Other than a meal which resulted in tasty bits of turkey, I had expected tomorrow, Thanksgiving Day, to come and go with little excitement.

Little did I know, I had a huge surprise coming.

Chapter 14

Clouds of mist blanketed the Mississippi the next morning as I peered out our fourth-story window. I'd completed my morning stretches when Daisy and Buddy roamed into the living room. They lifted their heads and twitched their noses following the scent of the turkey Izzie was stuffing. Buddy and I'd been in the kitchen last night while she mixed cornbread, celery and onions in a large bowl. One of the eggs she cracked for the dressing slipped right out of its shell and fell to the floor. Poor Momma. Not to worry, Buddy rubbed his tongue around his lips and hurried over to assist in the clean-up. Jake was handy with damp paper towels.

Izzie opened the oven door and approached it with the turkey filled roaster. We were lucky she had set it on an oven rack when a beating on the door made Izzie jump. The sound brought Jake to his feet. Izzie gasped and slid the turkey into the oven with a jerky motion, avoiding a dropped bird.

Jake opened the door to find Miss Leona crying, her lower lip quivering, a trait she revealed when unable to control her feelings.

"Oh, Jake. I'm here to tell you, Miss Gracie Lou's dead. Dead, I tell you. Dead as a door nail."

"What happened?"

"I really don't know. When I noticed she hadn't picked up her morning Memphis Times I thought I'd take it in to her. Her newspaper laid in the hallway all day yesterday. It just wasn't like Miss Gracie Lou, she always got her paper by noon.

"There she sat in her recliner, I thought, asleep. I went to her, touched her arm, it fell down to her side. Scared the bejesus out of me. Oh, Izzie, she was for sure, dead. And on Thanksgiving Day. Cheryl and the family coming. Harry's calling 9-1-1. I left to hurry up here to tell you all."

I cocked my head to listen. I needed Buddy to hear this too, but there he was behind the sectional with Daisy, the two snoring in unison. I realized I'd need to put on my thinking cap, that's what Izzie says, and pay attention 'cause I sure couldn't count on any help from Buddy or the Princess

"Was anything disturbed? Anything out of place?" Izzie asked.

"Nothing, I noticed. Well, there was one thing. Her bed pillow was on the floor beside her. Other than the pillow, everything seemed as neat as always. Wait, there were a couple coke cans on her side table and now that I think about it, she hadn't opened the FedEx package on the pink tufted loveseat inside her hallway."

Her description of the scene sounded vaguely familiar. I experienced a chilling sense of da-ja-vu and felt one of those rare moments when you think, 'I've heard this before'. Immediately, I was brought back to the scene of Clarabelle. She was found in her Lazy-Boy, a bed pillow, even soda cans, on the floor beside her. Her suspected killer was thought to be Uncle Jessie, but he'd have no grievance against Miss Gracie Lou. Or, would he?

Izzie frowned, "I'll call Cheryl. I hate to tell her daughter about his over the phone, especially on Thanksgiving, but there's no other way. You go on back downstairs. Jake can go with you. I'll come down after I make the call."

Izzie's voice was controlled, yet hesitant when she made the call. She explained the information Miss Leona had shared. "You talked to her last night? Did she sound okay? Did she mention having company? About what time was it? You had already planned to drive up to spend Thanksgiving with your Mom? We're not sure. Miss Leona found her this morning about seven-thirty when she went in with the newspaper. It had been outside her front door all day yesterday."

Izzie held the phone in one hand as she rubbed the back of her neck. She shook her head sideways, frowned and said, "Okay. You think you'll be here in about an hour? We'll watch for you. I'm so sorry for your loss."

Izzie frowned as she pressed the magic button so we could make the trip downstairs. During the ride down I remembered Miss Gracie Lou loved winning the Mah Jongg game. Those days were over. I wiggled my bottom, anxious to get off the elevator and examine the scene.

The door opened. Four paramedics were standing around. A fifth was with the body and, I suppose, declared her dead. I stood in the hallway next to Mr. Harry while questions were asked and answered, a lot of talking back and forth. Izzie pleaded with them to wait, not to move the body, until the daughter arrived. In response to Mr. Harry's 9-1-1 call the coroner arrived and pronounced her dead.

The paramedics decided to leave and let the funeral home pick up Miss Higgenbotham. They filed out in somber unison. Subdued funeral home attendants arrived and prepared to depart with their corpse.

I busied myself going room to room sniffing for any smell out of the ordinary. I'd learned from my Perry Mason School of Investigation to look for the little things. There was something. Maybe a clue.

It was nothing I had found. It was more like something I smelled. Something about the unpleasant muskiness frightened me. I knew that smell from somewhere. My hair bristled, my heart did that thumping it does when I'm on alert, not sure what it was, but I wanted out of there.

I ran out and into the entrance hall where Izzie was talking to Miss Leona.

"You asked," Miss Leona's lip again quivered, "if I'd noticed anything unusual. Well, I did notice something out of character for her. She'd been getting several FedEx deliveries lately. The ones she had to sign for. The same fellow, you know, the one who brings the package to the door, never left hers by her door. Not him. He always went inside, I guess to get a signature."

The scene was hard to shake from my mind as we pressed the magic button, waiting for our little room to appear.

Izzie said, "Here's the elevator, Sammy." I dashed inside, happy it was ready to take us upstairs. Jake stayed down with Miss Higgenbotham's daughter who'd arrived while I inspected the scene.

The elevator door was about to close when Miss Leona put her hand out to stop it from shutting. "I forgot to tell you, don't worry about a tenant for Miss. Higgenbotham's unit. I had a nice middle-age single man come in just last week looking for a unit. I'll call him, so don't you worry, honey, I'll have it rented in no time."

I thought, at last we had some good news, or did we?

Chapter 15

B uddy waited at the front door for us to return. We had a lot to cogitate about my snooping downstairs. We ran into the laundry area for our dog-speaking. Daisy couldn't have cared less. She had her chewy bone to work on. She was never going to be a detective. I supposed it was okay since she was a princess now.

While we were downstairs, Buddy said he and Daisy had visitors. Jake came in from downstairs as Izzie checked the pop-up on the roasting turkey. She picked up a piece of paper from the granite counter and yelled to Jake. "Hey, Jake, can you believe this?"

"What is it?"

"I found this note on the kitchen counter."

She read, "'Izzie, there was so much confusion on the first floor we came up, had a drink and are now leaving. We wouldn't want to put you out. I suppose you'll be too busy to fool with a meal for us so we're going to the club. Left the sweet potato pie in the fridge. Happy Thanksgiving, Mother.'"

"Well, I'll be damned. I never saw them, did you?" asked Jake.

Izzie plopped onto the sectional, put her feet on the coffee table and said, "No, I did not see them. They probably went up on the garage elevator. Let's pour some wine and wait for Hannah. I've had enough of Mother for one day."

Other than my heartache regarding Miss H's death, it hadn't been such a bad Thanksgiving. Olivia wasn't there to keep us guessing about what mood she'd be in and there were plenty of leftovers. My pals and I enjoyed turkey treats for several days that cold November.

Chapter 16

Monday of the next week had been a different story. That was the day planned for the memorial service for, Miss Gracie Lou Higgenbotham. Although the body hadn't been released, her daughter, Cheryl, wanted the service while the family was still visiting for Thanksgiving.

Jake and Buddy left for the ranch in Nesbit as soon as Jake finished his morning coffee saying they would be home later in the evening. Buddy had his morning rawhide chew to eat during the drive. Izzie hurried to take me and Daisy for our morning walk before Olivia arrived. It seemed this was not to be one of our GO days—at least for Daisy and me.

Izzie sat, on the black iron bench in the courtyard, bundled up against the wind while we took care of our nature calls. I understood her to say I was to watch Daisy while she and Olivia went to the memorial service for our beloved Miss Higgenbotham. No need to answer her, Izzie doesn't dog-speak

The kitchen cuckoo chirped nine-thirty as Olivia flounced through the front door. She never knocked. She had her own key and used it always at her convenience, not Izzie's. Olivia looked stunning with her blonde hair swept back on one side, leaving the other side to flow over her shoulder onto a maroon cashmere suit. A matching turtleneck sweater could be seen inside the lapels.

I wasn't surprised to see her because Miss Gracie Lou Higgenbotham was one of her dearest Mah Jongg ladies. Although several years older than Olivia, Miss Gracie Lou was a fierce player, known to count her winning quarters in front of the other players at the end of the days game. I've heard the ladies say her daughter, Cheryl, played the same way.

Sorry. I forgot. My mind wandered, typical these past years. Olivia arrived to attend the memorial service. I was sidetracked thinking about Olivia and the game she enjoyed with her dear dead friend.

Lowering herself gracefully onto the sofa, Olivia glanced sideways when Izzie came out of the bedroom. There was a feeling that engulfed me when I studied my sweet Momma. I nearly burst with pride to think how lucky I was to have her in my life. That day was one of those special days. She hadn't tripped over nor dropped anything. However, I admit to you, the day was still early.

Not yet thirty, Izzie showed off her flawless olive skin by wearing a sea green suit with just a touch of makeup. Her eyes were a different matter. She took a pencil and lightly drew around them, then, with a tiny, tiny brush, she fluffed her lashes. She smelled like gardenias, so good I could've licked her nose if she'd picked me up. The thought of being picked up on that day was out of the question. Momma and Olivia hurried toward the front door. No small talk, just deciding who would drive. Olivia was very bossy. She shook her keys in the air as they closed the front door. I suppose Olivia drove.

I was in the middle of one my dreams, about to catch the little mouse who insisted on teasing me by running under the pantry door, when the front door opened with a bang. Daisy barked. I jumped out of bed and ran to greet them, wagging my tail in welcome. I soon learned I should have stayed in my bed.

"The most ridiculous reception I've ever attended." Olivia said as they entered. "You would think Cheryl would have enough sense to put out a better spread than she did for us mourners. It's not like she couldn't afford it. Her mother left her plenty. No, she just didn't care about us grieving folks. Only thinks about herself. I'm sure she was raised better than that."

"Give it a rest, Mother. We didn't go for the food, did we? I thought we went to show respect for our friend."

"Respect, who's got respect, not that girl. I declare, I've never seen such a despicable spread in my life. She didn't even use her mother's sterling silver."

"Cheryl did bring her chocolate fudge cake with the hazelnut filling."

"I declare, Izzie, you know she already had made it for Thanksgiving."

"You really can't blame her, the funeral home catered it. The community room next to the chapel was lovely."

"Lovely? That is another thing. Whoever heard of having the reception at a funeral home. She could've had it downstairs at Gracie Lou's apartment. All those beautiful antiques just sitting there. Her daughter cares nothing for her mother's treasures. No one to enjoy them. Oh, I miss her already. All the fun times we had. Oh, my, oh, my."

"Yes, Mother, I understand, it must be difficult to lose a good friend, but we all must go sometime."

"I declare, this was not a good time for her to leave us. Izzie, I'm very concerned. She has died and left us in the lurch. Now we only have Leona, Judy, and me. Whoever will we get to take her place at the Mah Jongg tournament next week?"

"Yes, mother." Izzie answered sarcastically. "That is a real serious problem."

"Also, I'm wondering if you're ever going to find out any more about Mr. Cohen death? I don't like it. Another death, perhaps a murder, that one. It's been over two months and nothing more has been done. Nothing, I've heard. At least Jake has been doing his part supervising the changes so your sister and Patrick can move in."

As Izzie rolled her eyes heavenward she answered, "Oh. Lord, Mother, give it a break."

Chapter 17

I t was the first day of December, an unforgettable day. During the past year, I've played it over and over in my mind. The unpleasantness never fades. The day started out great, Momma cooked her favorite recipe of Ever Lovin' chili.

It was the day Patrick, released from therapy, should have begun his new teaching job at UT Memphis. Instead, he would be coming home in the afternoon to the loft he and Hannah had renovated, the loft designed with a nursery he'd never seen, the loft Hannah had modified to accommodate his wheelchair.

Izzie and Hannah talked last night over hot cocoa, deciding Hannah would go alone to pick him up. They agreed it best Jake should be waiting at the loft to assist with unloading the gear needed for Patrick's home rehabilitation. Walking was now a possibility, but many weeks of therapy would be needed to strengthen his back and leg muscles.

I scampered into the kitchen for my morning drink of water to find Izzie busily opening cans of beans. From the pot on the stove, I got a whiff of onion and beef. My saliva dripped on the floor in anticipation of the ground beef Momma placed in my bowl. The savory meat flavor tasted yummy. While Momma added the beans to her mixture, I went to Momma, nudged against her leg to let her know I loved her. Her pat on my head let me know she felt the same.

Jake and Buddy didn't make it home last night. Jake called to say they would be late coming home today because some cattle had broken out. The fence had to be repaired before he could leave. He was expected around noon, still in time to eat Momma's Ever Lovin' Chili and help Patrick get settled.

"Sammy, come here. We haven't had a run in a couple of weeks. After days like the past ones we've experienced, I need a jog even in these freezing temperatures," Izzie snapped on my red fleece-lined coat. She zipped her parka, pulled on a knitted cap, grabbed her gloves and we were off. A blast of cold fall air smacked my nose as we rushed into the early morning for our jog.

I enjoyed our time outside together, breathing the clean fall air. My short legs trotted as I ran next to her, matching her rhythmic pace. Daisy, four years older than me, was not at all skilled in the running game. We had left her to visit Leona and Harry. She and Leona walked at what I called the sniffing pace. This means Daisy sniffed every bush she came upon. It wasn't a good exercise to build heart rate, but the walk was still exercise for a twelve-year old Princess.

My heart pounded as Izzie removed my coat on the ride up. She was removing hers in our hall when the front door buzzer rang. After peeking through the little eye window, Izzie hesitated before opening the door. In walked Mr. Charcoal Grey Suit and Mr. Midnight Blue Suit.

Why were they here? They were polite enough, but a smile would have cracked the face of Agent Grey Suit. Instead of tea, Sweet Momma offered coffee. No takers. Everyone walked into the living room. At least I didn't have to listen to his squeaky, nasal questions because Agent Blue Suit started the conversation.

"Thank you for letting us in."

I thought – like she had a choice. At that moment I spied my arch nemesis as he wiggled his pointed mouse nose at me while he peeked from the opened pantry door. That little devil. I was too busy now to give him any attention.

Blue Suit raised his eyebrows and explained, "We need to speak with you and Jake regarding the reappearance of Jessie DeLisle. This is in connection with the case we are conducting against the Cohen estate for violation of the IRS Code regarding nonpayment of taxes."

Grey Suit added, "In doing so, we hope to locate your Uncle Jessie, alias Jerry Devilin."

Izzie gasped. "A connection? You think he's alive? Do you have any proof? He tried to kill me."

What, Jerry Devilin? I wanted to ask, but, of course, they could not have answered. They didn't know dog-speak.

What had happened to the investigation concerning Mr. Cohen?

I was on full alert as the Special Agents talked. Princess Daisy was asleep. Momma rubbed the nape of her neck. I jumped up beside her to give her a sense of calm. I wished Jake were home to help me watch over Momma. Thank goodness Grey Suit was quiet most of time.

"The Bureau believes it is time you knew more about your uncle's disappearance."

Izzie shook her head sideways. "I didn't realize there was anything else to know. Last week we called on some of the clubs where he used to play but learned nothing new. We presumed your ideas about him being alive were wrong.

"After the explosion, we determined Jessie, your uncle, floated to shore and contacted a gambling pal. This friend who came to his aid may have been Mr. Abram Cohen. This is being verified at this time."

"He, in turn, found a doctor who specialized in burns, also to do facial plastic surgery and scar revision to approximate a normal appearance. This reconstruction changed Mr. DeLisle's face, although still leaving one ear badly scared. We have facts to prove he spent six months after the surgery in Missouri with other gambling friends who were willing to give him sanctuary. The healing of his damaged ear and especially jawbone had to be supervised by a trained specialist, like ones who practice here in Memphis. This healing process has now taken nearly a year."

Agent Grey Suit snorted as he took a breath and said, "It is only alleged your neighbor, Mr. Cohen, gave him assistance."

"Our neighbor, Mr. Cohen?" Momma crumbled backwards in her chair. I wiggled in her lap while she inhaled a deep breath and squeezed me so tightly I thought I would pop.

Grey Suit snorted again and continued, "Mr. Cohen has for the past ten years owned a training facility for Black Russian Terriers in Germantown. These are in stables once owned by the Holiday Inn heiresses. The area is a compound of brick stables and out-buildings. In one of these side buildings he also managed high stakes gambling. This is where the bureau comes in.

We have concluded it was during your uncles' time of recovery Mr. Cohen came up with the idea of having Jessie, alias Jerry, oversee several of his illegal operations. This opportunity provided a safe haven for your uncle. It also allowed him to pay back his friend for his financial support and contacts during his reconstructive surgery and recovery.

The black Russian terrier Training facility bred puppies which easily sold for as much as twenty-five-thousand dollars. The kennels had a stellar reputation. The unique training offered there brought in a celebrity customer who spared no expense, up to forty-thousand dollars, to ensure their puppies were trained to the highest standards."

My sweet Momma stared with a fixed gaze as the agent spoke. I pushed against her and scooted between her hip and the arm of the chair. I knew by the shake of her head she was surprised to hear Uncle Jessie could be alive and under surveillance. Talk about being surprised. It took me more than a few minutes to realize he was saying terriers, not terrorists.

"Jessie popped up on our radar when the doctor who did the scar revision notified authorities," said Blue Suit.

Blue Suit said, "Jessie-Jerry, is wanted for the murder of your father, Matt. He is also the principal person-of-interest in the death of the DeLisle housekeeper, Clarabelle, and Father Sims, the Catholic priest. These two victims have now been added to the list after several interviews. Using various investigative techniques to obtain evidence, The Bureau began working with local law enforcement. We are now certain he was also responsible for the killing and dismemberment of a young Caruthersville man thirty years ago. At this time, we have some knowledge of his location because your new maintenance man whom the Applegate's hired two months ago is one of our special agents."

Then came what humans call the kicker. Shock and disbelief showed on Izzie's face when they revealed two months earlier Jessie-Jerry had stayed a few nights across the hall with Mr. Cohen. I licked her hand and rubbed my head against her leg to comfort her. The maintenance man agent witnessed a late-night argument on a weekend when Izzie, Jake, and we dogs were in Nesbit. After a heated exchange, they suspect Jessie was not a welcome guest. He left the next day after only being on the premises a few nights.

"You found Mr. Cohen's body a couple days later," said Grey Suit.

"Stop. Are you are telling me Jessie was here, living across the hall?" Izzie wrapped her arms around me and rocked back and forth. Her body trembled as she continued. "Why wasn't I told?"

"Madam, this period of time when the information started to come together was last summer when you were living in Nesbit, Mississippi. Leaking evidence to you or your family would have blown the cover of our agent. He was here to protect you and the other tenants."

"Protect? Well, your agent did a piss-poor job of it. He let Mr. Cohen be murdered, and who knows, maybe Miss Higgenbotham as well."

"Please, stay calm, Ms. DeLisle. We have everything under control now." Grey Suit paused, starring into space for a moment. "Although, there is a possibility Jessie could be the person responsible for the murder of both your tenants."

Izzie stood up so fast I nearly fell off my seat. "Jessie, another murder? Get out." She stomped toward the door and opened it so hard it bounced against the wall. "Get out, now."

The Special Agents shook their heads in stunned disbelief. They stood, obeyed Izzie's command and headed for the door just as Buddy dashed in with Jake behind him. For a split second everyone seemed to freeze in motion. There was complete silence.

"We understand this is a lot to process. But, understand, time is of the essence and we will be back." Grey Suit snorted as the door slammed behind them.

Izzie turned from the door, tears streaming down her pale face. I could have licked them dry, but Jake had the answer as he stepped toward her. His tight embrace quieted her trembles as she laid her head on his shoulder and sobbed.

Chapter 18

Jake talked to Momma softly as he rubbed her back. She continued to shake, sobbing quietly. Carefully, Jake swooped her up and carried her to their bedroom. I listened outside the door as Izzie, between gasps and sobs, told Jake about the visit from the federal agents.

I'd watched Momma's every movement. I'd heard fear in her voice. I suppose we all experience fear at one time or another. It gets a grip on you and doesn't let go. It grasps and twists our emotional and physical body until we are consumed by it. That is what those memories of Uncle Jessie did to my Momma. As I've reached my golden years, I've learned, after the fear is overcome, it's easy to see how foolish it might have been to begin with. I didn't think Momma was at that point yet. My heart ached for her.

As suddenly as Izzie had exploded to the agents, she was then unexpectedly quiet and subdued. Closing the door behind him, Jake walked to the kitchen and made a pot of coffee. Steam rose from the hot brew as he stared out the window to the river below. The woman he loved was suffering. I grasped the extent of his hurting, we both felt the frustration and defeat of being unable to lessen her pain.

What may have been hours flew by. It was late in the day. I remember there had been several cuckoos when I awoke. The ringing of Jake's cell phone interrupted my nap.

"Yes, Hannah. About twenty minutes. Okay. I'll be watching for you."

I gathered from what I'd heard, Patrick was on his way home. Jake and Buddy walked out our front door. I ran to catch up with them, leaving Daisy to care for the sleeping Izzie. I heard the elevator stop and its doors open. Buddy barked a welcoming woof-woof.

The last time I'd seen him, Patrick was a huge, muscular black man. This man getting off the elevator was thin, barely able to maneuver his wheelchair out of the elevator. Deep ridges lined his sunken cheeks. His hair, once black, now showed streaks of grey.

He smiled, speaking with an upbeat, though strained voice, "Good boy, Buddy." He gave Buddy an ear scratch and struggled to wheel himself forward. Jake and Buddy followed as Jake helped him maneuver his wheelchair forward.

Hannah unlocked the door to their loft, bent down and kissed her husband on the cheek, "Welcome home, darlin'".

All was quiet as Hannah closed the door. I turned and hoofed it toward our loft.

Several cuckoos later, Jake and Buddy opened the front door. They spied Sweet Momma and me, cuddled in her soft green recliner. My drowsy Momma's hair was a mess. Her body drooped as she sipped hot cocoa she'd made in the microwave. Jake walked to us, bent over and kissed Momma on the top of the head, then told her about getting Patrick settled.

I wanted to believe we were on our way to becoming a happy family. I soon learned, one can never be too sure of anything.

Chapter 19

Izzie sometimes would say time has a way of healing. I'm not so sure, but I believed time and necessity can make people creative in a way that could promote healing. Both sisters needed to heal. Both were resourceful. I had faith they were capable of handling all these problems. Murder of their neighbor, death of a friend, Patrick's health issues, and Uncle Jessie's possibly being alive and involved in all this. It was a lot to handle, even for them.

Two days after Patrick got settled in his routine, Hannah popped in to visit with Izzie. They talked about the information the agents shared on their last visit.

It was during their conversation Hannah said, "Hey, I may have a grand idea. Those agents told you about the Black Russian Terriers. I've read several articles about BRTs. They're wonderful service dogs. They can be taught to turn on light switches, pick up items off the floor, and even push a wheelchair."

"So, are they kind of a therapy dog too?"

"Sure. I'd say so. Don't you think Patrick would be more independent having a BRT? The dog could brace him when he goes from his wheelchair to bed or to the toilet or shower. So, I'm thinking we should go out to Germantown, inspect the kennels like I need a dog for Patrick, which I may. Who knows? It would give us a chance to look the place over and maybe pick-up some hints about this IRS/Jessie situation."

Izzie answered, "Do you think it's safe? After all, they may all be crooks."

"You said the Agents referred to illegal gambling, not raising dogs."

"But, that's just a front," said Izzie.

"Listen to me. There may be big-time gambling on the property but that doesn't mean other people don't go there for this special breed of dogs. I think we should go." Hannah insisted.

"Well, I suppose you're right. Patrick may truly need a service dog."

"He's been having nightmares since he got home. Can you imagine what it will be like, getting up in the night for him as well as a baby? With our baby due in May, a BRT could keep Patrick occupied and perhaps be a calming force in his daily life."

Izzie tilted her head back and laughed, "You may be right, or you could end up with two babies."

"Leave that to me," said Hannah. "Let's go this afternoon while the rehab therapist is here giving Patrick his daily workout."

Chapter 20

Promptly at cuckoo one Hannah tapped on the door and we were off for the Black Russian Terrorist, I mean, terrier kennels. The Princess got to go too. She was so happy she jumped and wiggled while we waited for the elevator.

I, on the other hand, was composed, knowing my job for the day was to control the Princess if she got overly excited. Perhaps, to protect my Momma, too, should she be faced with a problem from possible crooks.

"Do you think it wise to take both Shih Tzus?"

Izzie turned to Hannah, "Not to worry. When Sammy and Daisy are together, she follows him everywhere, doing everything he does. With Buddy, that's another story. Anything can happen with that Lab."

We were thankful Buddy was out for the day with Jake. I noticed the sisters had on matching trench coats, prepared for the drizzle which could turn into a cold November rain at any moment.

Izzie opened the back-car door for us to jump into our doggie seats. I did as was expected, knowing Daisy would follow. She did. I gave her a good girl wink. Izzie drove east on I-240 past the airport. According to Hannah we made the thirty-five-minute drive in twenty-five. It was either light traffic or, as Hannah said, Izzie's heavy foot.

Izzie's feet never appeared at all heavy to me. I'd always thought she had dainty feet. Clumsy, but dainty. Hannah, just the opposite of her sister, drives the speed of a turtle I used to see on the back roads of Olivia's ranch. Slow and steady. Funny thing. Izzie's never been in a wreck. Hannah's had three. I was glad my Momma drove that day.

Wow, I was taken aback by the size of the kennels. Huge brick barns, surrounded by all sorts of holly bushes, tall and short, that looked amazing as we drove up the driveway. When Izzie opened the car door for us, I caught a glimpse of red cardinals darting among the red berries of the hollies. A beautiful sight. The front and largest of four buildings had been stables back in the 1970s explained Hannah.

As we walked toward the double sliding door, Hannah reminded Izzie these were the stables where she took riding lessons as a teenager. The two Wilson sisters, daughters of Kemmons Wilson, founder of the Holiday Inn chain, owned and trained hunters and jumpers there. Momma, never the horsewoman, slid the double front door open and walked in without comment.

This doorway led into a short hallway with glass paneled offices on either side. On the rough-sawed wooden walls hung a sign, 'Work is the master key that opens the door to all opportunities'-Kemmons Wilson.

A smiling lady with grey hair slid back her glass panel to ask if we had an appointment. So, what, I thought. We were just here to look at a dog, not visit a vet. I supposed they were particular who got in to see those expensive dogs.

She was making sure all visitors were there to see BRTs. After we explained our intent was to see the dogs, she called a couple young ladies from the office across the hall who came out to greet and guide us through the kennel.

Let me tell you this. It was a cold fall day. The wind outside howled as we walked into the kennels but these young women, Robin and

Marianne, had on midriffs cut so low I'd have thought we were at the beach. Just my opinion. I'd say they were there for more than directing people to see a bunch of puppies.

Daisy and I scurried to keep up with Momma and Miss Marianne. Hannah walked ahead with Miss Robin. She told us about the breed as we approached rooms the size of horse stalls which is what she said they'd been.

Abruptly Daisy and I froze in our tracks. Before us was the largest animal I'd ever seen to be called a dog. I knew they must be mistaken. She was showing us ponies. Yet, I thought, never had I seen a black curly pony with curls hanging over its eyes.

While my thoughts were going haywire, Little Daisy began a low, deep growl. She even scared me. Izzie extended her hand, palm out which meant 'stop'. No stopping Daisy. She showed her teeth. I lurched forward to take control. Brushing next to her I pushed all ten pounds of her trembling body out of sight of the beast that scared her. Poor Princess Daisy, she needed me to teach her so many things. How to be brave was one of many.

Our guide said, "I've been with these dogs for five years and love every-one. BRTs adore being around people. We begin socializing them during the first week after birth. It's a positive step toward training your dog because they love being around people and enjoy the companionship that comes with training. However, we must guard against them becoming too protective of their owner. Anything different in their world could be a cause for them becoming too shielding."

I began to think this Miss Robin may not know how to dress but she sure knows her Russians.

She continued, "In this stall we have four puppies ready to go to their forever homes. There were nine in this litter. They were about the size of a big baking potato when born. The bitch had an easy birth and licked each one over and over. She sired five beautiful females and four males.

"The girls now weigh about twenty pounds. The male puppy weighs right at twenty-five pounds. They eat between one to two pounds of raw meat in the morning then another one to two pounds in the evening. Along with the raw meat they receive four to six cups of kibble daily. They have had all their shots and their pedigree can be registered with the AKC should you wish."

"What," asked Hannah, "is your opinion of them as service dogs? I've read they are magnificent working with the handicapped."

"One female from this litter went to a blind eight-year old. Her parents appear excited with the progress the child and dog have made. You must realize this breed of dog was bred to be guards for the Soviet Red Army. They are very intelligent and excel as service and therapy dogs."

Hannah walked close to the stall and knelt down to reach threw the gate to yaps of welcome and wet licking tongues. "They are so cuddly. Watch how cute they are as they climb over each other."

"Would you like to go in the pen with them?"

Hannah squealed at the idea and approached the furry beasts.

Izzie stayed back, talking to Marianne, while Daisy and I hovered in a corner away from those bear-like black beasts with sloppy wet tongues. I wondered what Buddy would think of such an animal.

Chapter 21

"Are you sure?" Izzie asked Hannah as we loaded into the car. I cocked my head so my good ear could pick-up their words.

"I'll talk to Patrick this evening about it, but yes, I'm sure it's what we need. We can both go to the training sessions, but it will be Patrick's dog to brush, take on walks and feed. I think he will realize his companion relies on him as much as he will rely on the dog. We're still not sure if the injuries are permanent."

Izzie answered. "Let's hope the doctors know soon. In the meantime, going on walks in his chair should be no challenge. Down the elevator, out the front door, through the courtyard and on to Riverside Drive. Thank goodness y'all got moved before the accident. How are you holding up, Sis? Over your morning sickness yet?"

"I'm through the first trimester, so I'm in a good place now. Those runs to the bathroom have nearly stopped. Patrick's teaching position has been put on hold until the next semester. There are some things we need for the nursery but no hurry. I was disappointed today. I was hoping we'd get a clue regarding the gambling the Agents talked about, but nothing. Yes, a puppy would work wonders to keep our spirits up."

"Well, it'll be a great Christmas present," said sweet Momma. "Which one did you like the best?"

"Oh, the male definitely. I told Miss Robin that Patrick and I would drive out Sunday to see if we are a fit. I left a hundred-dollar deposit for the male puppy, all twenty-five pounds of him. I'm going to talk to Patrick, have him mention how this dog is a gamble, not the kind of gambling he usually likes. Maybe something will come from his conversation, you think?"

I woofed to Daisy. She could have asked our opinion before making such a rash decision. My life was about to change. Again.

Chapter 22

S unday dawned sunny and clear with a slight breeze rolling off the river. My nose got an earthy whiff of dried leaves as they crunched under my paws when I answered nature's call. Buddy entertained himself chasing the squirrel that had teased him for the last two years, while Daisy took her time smelling every bush in the courtyard, trying to decide where to land her morning deposit. I, on the other hand, had more pressing issues before me.

I heard Izzie tell Jake after she pressed the magic button that today was the day our family might increase. Hannah didn't have much of a bump yet, so I surmised they could only be talking about the black curly beast. I was referring to the so called dog we'd met yesterday when I had to take charge in order to rescue Princess Daisy.

I was perplexed about the situation facing me that day. There was one, possibly two murders to solve, plus the added burden of training the black beast should he join our family. All this to be done with no help from Daisy or Buddy. I had learned not to expect much from Daisy, considering her being an heiress and all, but Buddy?

Now that was a different story. I finally spotted him as he followed Mr.

Squirrel to the back side of the old oak and began to bark his fool head off. No one paid any attention until Izzie's phone rang.

"Come on. You three will have a new friend in about an hour. We need to get upstairs and get ready to greet him."

Oh, brother, it was true. I shook off the leaves from my clean fur and ran to catch up. I might as well make the most of it. Daisy wasn't so bad after I got used to her. Maybe this young scamp would be a fast learner. At least, he'd be sleeping across the hall. It was bad enough I, early on, had to share my bed with Daisy. This new black beast could take up my entire bed.

Chapter 23

No more had we hopped off the elevator than Izzie gathered some of my chewy treats and we headed back down to the courtyard. We started to play fetch when I glanced up to see the black beast being taken out of Patrick's SUV in a crate. His big black eyes peeped first at me, like two shiny black rocks. He then starred at everyone. Jake went toward the garage to assist with Patrick and his wheelchair while Hannah carried the crate a little closer. She slowly bent over and opened the crate door.

Like a bolt of lightning that puppy critter bounded toward us knocking Hannah to the ground. Man was he fast. Izzie ran to her sister, helped her stand. They brushed off old dried leaves from Hannah's tan trench coat and laughed.

That puppy didn't walk, he trotted. Then he began a gallop round and round the courtyard. Maybe he was part horse. He sure was the size of a young pony. Buddy joined in the run with little Daisy way far behind. I started to put a stop to this frolicking but thought better of it as the beast headed toward me. Crash. That giant puppy tripped over me and down we went.

Now, you know the story of how I met Nickie. He would, as the years passed, become my bestest friend next to Buddy. His full name was Nicholai Roberto Jones. Saint Nicholas, the Wonderworker, was the patron saint of children, sailors, merchants, prostitutes, and students. An odd patron if you ask me, but Nickie was a Christmas present to everyone, so I guess the name suited him. I remember thinking it noteworthy St. Nicholas was born December 6, the day Nickie came to live with our family. I wasn't much of a praying dog, but on that day, I prayed this was a good omen.

He was a smart young pup and quickly learned to open doors for Patrick. To train him they would tie a towel on the door handle, one of those sideways handles, shake it and give the command. When Nickie pulled on the towel and the door opened Patrick rewarded him with a treat and praise. He stayed so close to Patrick you would think they were glued together.

St. Nicholas was well known for dropping presents at children's homes. By the time Nickie reached full growth of one hundred fifty-eight pounds two years later, you would not believe the size of the deposit he left every morning in our courtyard.

I still remember after all those years, Hannah called his morning deposits, a five bagger.

Chapter 24

"I wanted you and Hannah to know the new tenant moved into 1-B yesterday after you all had gone upstairs with the new dog. I knew you were busy with the pup, so I thought there was no need to tell you then."

It was Monday, the day after Nickie moved in to be Patrick's companion. Miss Leona brought us a rhubarb pie and shared the information.

"Did everything go alright?" Izzie asked.

"Oh, yes. He paid his deposit and three months in advance in cash. I'll go to the bank today, unless you're going. Harry said we shouldn't keep that much cash around."

"No, you go. I'm due at the hospital for an all-day shift. Did you find out what he does for a living?" Izzie asked.

"On the rental application he said he was retired. He and two helpers unloaded the U-Haul in no time flat. Didn't have much furniture, but a lot of technical stuff, like computers and a couple guitars. Bedroom furniture, bookcases, and a large desk, maybe a sofa and that was it. Very quiet fellow, he is."

"Let me know if he needs anything. Miss Gracie Lou had been with us for so many years, it's difficult to imagine anyone else living there."

"Okay. Will do."

"What have you heard about Miss Higgenbotham death?" Izzie asked. "Did the police question you anymore?"

"No. Nothing. I wonder if it was natural causes."

"Probably. Could have been. She was in her eighties." said Izzie. "Do let me know how Mr. …What did you say his name was?"

"James Devour. He's not from around here, he said."

I'd been listening to Izzie's conversation as we four dogs played snatch-the-ball from Buddy. Something I heard interested me, caused me to stop playing, go to my bed and do some deep dog-thinking. James Devour, Jerry Devilin, Jessie DeLisle. Probably just a coincidence. Still, my hair bristled digesting this information.

Chapter 25

T he aroma of fresh brewed coffee awakened me the next morning. The specific aroma was nutty and smoky, probably the kind Jake gets from those black beans in the burlap bags. We dogs gathered in the kitchen waiting our morning feed. Steam from Izzie's cup drifted upward stirring something in my brain that made me feel content. I was enjoying my happy place when Izzie's phone rang.

Still in her Victoria's Secret chenille bathrobe covered with flowers and hearts, Izzie said, "Sure, come on over."

Before I could drink a good morning swallow from my water bowl, the door opened with a bang. In popped Nickie, Patrick, and Hannah. Patrick rolled his chair next to the table. Nickie bounced over to Buddy. A lot of sniffing went on while Princess Daisy and I watched.

Patrick was talking. "It was an out-of-the-ordinary experience yesterday. This man, J.D. showed us around the kennel, answered all our questions with considerable knowledge of the breed. I was conscious of a slight head jerk when I mentioned gambling. I told him, in my condition, I preferred betting on a sure thing more so than raising a dog. Hannah and I were there nearly two hours, did a lot of talking about nothing in particular but, as time wore on, he became increasingly friendly."

Hannah interrupted, "I thought the men might make a better connection without me around. I left them alone for most of the time and talked to Miss Robin, who I might add, was more covered than she had been before."

"This J.D. guy and I discussed the advantages of buying a pup and training him myself rather than buying a fully trained adult dog. To completely train a service dog requires at least twenty-four hours. We could start with the basics at the Center. Then I could work with him, and later come back in a few months for further professional training. The initial purchase cost would be much less, and we would develop a strong bond as I trained him. These would be good reasons to gamble on a pup rather than to buy an adult dog.

Patrick continued, "Black Russians are smart and catch on to their training very fast. They develop a very close bond with their owners and prefer to take orders only from them. Anyway, when we signed the papers and so forth, J.D. suggested I bring Nickie back this Wednesday at three-thirty for some special training getting him used to commands I'd use for the chair. We should have the basics down in a month or so.

"He believes, BRTs do best when training starts much earlier than most breeds. I said 'great, would look forward to it'. Then, he said one of the young ladies would also work with him at each visit. There would still be some time for a poker game."

"Man, you've done great. Sounds like he might check you out for a short impromptu game. Either way, you may be on to a lead. Congrats. And, on the dog too." Jake said.

Izzie quizzed. "Did you see any others or get any hint Uncle Jessie might be around?"

"Not by me." Hannah answered.

Patrick hesitated. "I want to get in on that game. Jake, you'll need to go with me. I'll try to size up the players. Also, someone has to run the game. I bet we could find out more tomorrow when Nickie and I go to the kennel."

It always surprised me the amount of information I could acquire by just listening.

Chapter 26

A blustery wind off the Mississippi blew my ears back as Jake took me, Princess Daisy, Buddy, and Nickie for our morning hike. This was the first morning since returning from the hospital that Patrick decided to stay inside. He was determined to save his strength for the upcoming trip to the kennels. Daisy and I stayed snug and warm in our matching red fleece coats while Buddy and Nickie looked warm enough with their God-given fur. Jake headed for the dog park on Riverside to let us run off leash.

Daisy and I followed Jake's brisk pace, paying attention to not slip on scattered patches of sidewalk ice. Inside the doggie park, Buddy and Nickie lunged at each other like two puppies. It's true one was a puppy though he was now twice my size. He seemed to sprout an inch or two every day.

He ran, no, he galloped around us in a mad frenzy of excitement. Buddy soon tired of playing and was content to walk through the park with the rest of us. We were all content to follow Jake's fast pace on our walk home. We entered our building as Harry Applegate was leaving 1-A with four treats. A cold, but happy group we were as we grabbed our treats and ran toward the elevator.

We bolted out of our floating room just as Patrick closed his apartment door and rolled toward us. The elevator door stood open as Patrick rolled inside. Nickie turned and followed close behind. Jake opened the front door of our loft for me, Daisy, and Buddy to run inside. Not me. I hopped back on the elevator just as the door was closing.

Patrick laughed. "What a scrapper you are. Hitching a ride with us. You'd better watch out, Nickie, or you'll have a friend with you on your first day of training."

Patrick was more right than he knew at that time.

He rolled toward his SUV, stopping on the passenger side. Jake, Nickie, and I were close behind when all of a sudden I felt my paws were wet. Jake slipped sideways and fell against the car.

"What the hell?" Jake yelled.

"What is it, man?" Patrick answered.

"There's oil running from under your car. Could your oil pan have sprung a leak?"

Patrick twisted his body in the chair to look to the concrete floor. A black, greasy liquid was running from under the frame. "Don't think so. We haven't been on any rocky roads."

"Well, this is a disaster," said Jake. "We're lucky Nickie didn't get in this mess. Let's go back upstairs. I'll carry my oily shoes and Sam. Izzie can bath him while I contact Paul's Auto Shop for a service call. Hopefully, he can send a man out right away. Can you call the kennels to let them know there is a problem?"

"Sure."

Jake held me with a tight grip under my tummy. I knew better than to squirm in a situation like this. My paws, especially the front ones, were beginning to burn as he handed me to Izzie and went into the kitchen. He poured himself steaming hot coffee in his Starbuck's mug and dialed. Then, he left the apartment.

Izzie removed my red fleece, carried me, feet pointed away from her, into the laundry room. She began a massive clean-up by gently rubbing a smelly liquid on my paws, then a great suds and scrub. I confess I felt better after Momma completed my clean-up. A red and white checked neck scarf completed my dapper look. The oil mess turned out great for me.

One cuckoo later, Jake came back to tell us the bolt on the oil pan had been the problem. It was just loose causing a slow leak that had probably been dripping over-night. The service man tightened the pan and said he'd send another guy out to clean the garage floor. We loaded up and took off again.

Patrick, with Jake's help, had a system for loading the wheelchair in the SUV. That system meant neither guy paid much attention to us dogs. From his first car ride, Nickie started to develop a weird habit, one that only got worse with time. He would not, I mean, he would never, load from the passenger side. He would stand beside the driver's back door until it was opened, hop in and lay across the seat, taking up much of the surface, leaving little room for anyone else, especially me.

Not to worry, on that day I jumped in behind him and lay undetected on the floor behind the driver's seat, practically unnoticed, hidden by the grey bath towel on the floorboard. Well, it worked. Patrick shut the back door, then with Jake's help got in the front passenger side. Jake attached the chair to the frame on the back of the SUV. He got in the driver's seat. We were ready to roll. As we pulled out of the underground garage I scrunched on to the back seat beside Nickie and peered out the back window. Only then did Jake realize what I'd done. Oh, yes, he saw me. He and Patrick laughed. Not a problem.

We were on our way to experience Nickie's first training lesson and to further my investigation to get information, if any was to be had, about possible gaming conducted at the black Russian terrier kennels.

Chapter 27

The massive brick barns came into sight as we exited the highway and started the drive up the gravel road. Holly bushes bearing red berries swayed in the wind luring cardinals and encouraging customers to drive forward. It was an enticing sight.

We unloaded. The wheels of Patrick's chair crunched on the pebbled path as Jake pushed its passenger toward the kennel. Nickie, on lead, tugged to walk faster. He sure needed training on proper walk technique. I trotted close to Jake, watching two cardinals dart in and out of a berry-laden holly bush. The sound of Jake's phone startled me.

I heard sweet Momma's voice. "Hi, Jake. Could you all be home by seven? Olivia just called and wanted to stop by with her friend for drinks. Since they missed us Thanksgiving Dinner because of the Higgenbotham death, she thought this visit might work."

"Sure, we'll do our best, although due to that oil leak fiasco we are running behind here."

Izzie continued, "Understood. Maybe this time we'll get to see his face, wonder if we'll recognize him from the yacht club."

Entering the main room of the kennel, we were greeted by a man who introduced himself as J.D. He reminded me of someone I'd seen in a movie on Izzie's TV. It took some deep dog thoughts to remember. Finally, it came to me. The movie was Titanic. The actor was Leonardo DiCaprio only much older with heavy rimmed glasses. He wore a ball cap tilted to his left side possibly making his face look misshapen. I tried to get him in balance but felt somehow his body, or perhaps just his face was distorted. He wore too much *Aramis* cologne. I'm very knowledgeable about men's cologne because last year I listened to Momma read me her Christmas present list.

We headed into a horse show ring, now converted into multiple areas where Russians were going through various commands. The J.D. man explained commands to Patrick and Nickie while Jake and I listened. After watching this for a while I decided I'd seen enough and trotted over to a side doorway. I stood there and had a look at the lay-out of the grounds. I needed to snoop around. Then I spied a pathway leading to two brick buildings a few feet from the side of the kennel. I'd started down the gravel path leading there, when abruptly Mr. J.D. surprised me from behind.

"Where ya think youse' going, Little Squirt?" He asked.

Not accustomed to being addressed in such a manner, I scurried on, paying Mr. J.D. no attention.

Behind him, Jake was pushing Patrick. We all were headed toward a black door of a building with black windows, maybe a window shade, not sure. I just noticed the windows were not clear glass like ours in the loft.

Two black Harley's were parked to the right side of the front door.

"Nickie's training today will take over an hour so I thought youse' guys might enjoy a little game I've got going on back here," J.D. said.

He opened a door into a semi-lit room filled with stale cigar smoke. I sniffed a woody, leathery musty smell. Someone was wearing Aramis. As we stepped into the room everyone turned toward us and froze. No sound was made.

An oblong poker table which could have seated eight players now only seated five. This group of men, and the table and chairs, took up the middle of the room. This allowed space for a small kitchenette on the left. Another door set between bookcases of rough boards, at the far right was closed. I studied the faces of the players. The first man I noticed looked slightly familiar.

An incandescent overhead bulb shone down on his bald head. The expression on his chubby face was pleasant as he smiled and reached down to give me a pat. To his left, a stern-faced burly man sported a red-tinted beard as he spit into a grimy Campbell soup can. To his left, a Stetson rested on the head of a tall freckled-faced cowboy.

Continuing around the circle sat an elderly man wearing a dark suit, white shirt unbuttoned at the neck, no tie. To his left was a shorter man dressed in all black. He wore wire rimmed glasses, a black swede skull cap and stared straight ahead. He reminded me of a younger version of Mr. Cohen. I knew all these men, but from where? It took me a few minutes of dog-think to remember where I'd seen those fellows.

Not a word was spoken until Mr. J.D. broke the silence saying, "Hey, mates. Here's two guys who needs' ta' let off some steam. I told them Texas Hold'em was the best way to do that. I'll pour youse' all a neat scotch."

He grabbed a chair for Jake and put it between The Suit and the Skull Cap and said, "here you go."

He pointed to an open spot for Patrick to pull up his wheelchair.

Patrick rolled his wheelchair up to the table and shook his hand, signaling 'no' to the drink offer. He, instead, paused a moment, then reached in his front pocket for what I recognized as a roll of green money. He held up two green bills which J.D. took and handed Patrick and Jake each a roll of poker chips.

J.D. sat down at Patrick's right as the dealer. He dealt each player two cards. The game had begun. I quickly hid under the table, hopefully to be unnoticed by the gamblers and to pay attention to any conversation which could help my dog-thinking.

Except for the smack of chips hitting the table, the room was quiet. The one overhead bulb shed little light except on to the table. It took me some time to realize another man, wearing sunglasses, was not playing but sitting in an office chair beside a small counter in the kitchen area.

The chubby-faced man, wearing a Cardinals sweatshirt, stood and walked over to Mr. Sunglasses. With a ballpoint pen he signed a piece of paper the man provided, then handed him two rolls of chips. When chubby face took his place, I heard the smack of chips as they hit the table.

I laid under the poker table and pondered about the players. The man in the skull cap was just beginning to give me a clue when a buzzer from the door disrupted me. Mr. Sunglasses rose from his chair and swaggered toward the sound. He walked outside and shut the door. By huddling close to the door, I could hear him grumble to someone outside.

Suddenly, the door burst open. "You gentlemen need anything? Chips? Drinks? I's got some fool-headed drunk out here, I need to attend to."

No one answered. He slammed the door as he went outside and began fuming, "Why in the hell are you bothering me? You won that damn pick-up from Mr. Cohen, not me. He's been dead over two months. You should've seen him before he died if you wanted your blasted truck title."

The other man's voice became shrill, "Besides the truck title, I gots' me another asshole who owes me six grand. I need help on this. I don't know what to do. I'm not a brawlin' kind'a guy."

"I might know a man who might know a man who for the right price can solve most problems."

"Don't you hook me up with one of youse' man-who-paints-houses. I don't need no hit man. Cohen's already dead."

"Listen, pal, he sure as hell is. Hear me now, Cohen didn't do right by me or some the other guys in there, neither. He was one cheap bastard but, I'm the kinda' guy who takes care of my own problems. I'll see what I can do for ya. Be in touch in a few days."

I lunged under the table as the door opened. Like a jolt, it hit me. The man in black, all of them, were at Mr. Cohen's memorial service. I wasn't so sure about the man wearing sunglasses.

Chapter 28

On the drive home, I thought about all the facts I'd gathered when I hid under the gaming table. My dog-think was difficult because of the deafening snoring that came from Nickie. He was asleep as soon as his head hit the car seat. From the sound coming from him one might think he was related to Buddy. He must have had a hard work-out.

I used to think Buddy was loud. I'd never heard the likes of loud snoring until the black beast arrived. Not only that, he stretched out on the back seat leaving me no room for my exhausted body. Dog-think can take a lot of mental energy. I needed to be comfortable. My solution was to make circles on the grey towel lying on the floor behind the driver's seat. I finished my circles, gave up and plopped down to do my dog-thinking. I'd need to run the facts by Buddy the moment we got home.

To some people Buddy might have seemed slow on the uptake, but he was the best silent partner a crime solver like me could have. He was quiet but always alert, always watching. True, his movements were usually slow, but man, if need be, Buddy was fast bounding forward to catch a criminal. I thought we might train Nickie in our skills of mystery-solving because he was beginning to show a keen skill of attentiveness. In addition, his size could be threatening. Still a puppy at forty-five pounds, he could scare the bejesus out of you. Just wait until he grew up.

Daisy was a lost cause. Her nickname, Princess, suited her quite well. She was a delicate looking Shih Tzu, fragile and petite, with flowing golden fur. Pretty to look at but, for sure, not qualities I needed in the complex situations of crime solving.

Hannah and Izzie were waiting for us as the elevator door opened. Patrick rolled into their loft. Nickie traipsed behind them without a look back at us. That young pup had experienced a strenuous training session. His droopy eyes told me his nap wasn't over.

Izzie gave me a scratch on my ear and Jake a tight hug. "You're home in the nick of time. Hope you boys had a good day. Mother and her date should be here any minute. I've prepared cocktail sauce for the prawns Mother loves so well."

She turned toward Jake, smiling a flirty grin. "I'm ready to bake a Brie in apricot pastry just for you. It's the large one from Sam's so you can share," she said teasingly.

Jake grabbed her around the waist and kissed her on the top of her head.

"I'll take a fast shower. See you in a few minutes. Man, what a day. Tell you all about it later." Jake said as he hurried through the door headed for the bathroom.

Buddy, Daisy, and I rushed to our food bowls. We bumped each other as we scurried toward Izzie while she poured our kibble. It was nearly a clean pour until Buddy, in his excitement, bumped Momma, causing her to drop his bowl. Kibble went everywhere. Not a problem. Buddy ate it as fast as Izzie tried to pick it up. Daisy's and mine had been served first, paired with beef liver. Glad she'd served us first. Of course, Daisy grabbed each bite and carried it to the kitchen rug.

The doorbell buzzed as Jake appeared, handsome as earlier, only now smelling more of *Gucci* than cigar smoke. Jake's black short-cropped beard was neat as his collar-length black waves. He wore starched jeans and a navy plaid shirt, his usual wardrobe. I've heard Momma say he wears tapered shirts to show off his powerfully built body. To be honest, I'd never noticed.

Jake paid no attention to Patrick, Hannah, and Nickie as they came in the front door. He sneaked up behind Izzie, gently hugged my sweet Momma in a loving embrace and planted a big kiss on her neck. Love is so grand.

Chapter 29

Nickie strutted to the sectional and sprawled out taking up more space than was his fair share. Hannah pointed her index finger toward the floor saying, "down". The black beast's ears perked, he gave her a sideways glance and jumped off the furniture. That was one smart pup.

Patrick maneuvered his wheelchair into a position for conversation. Izzie put out crackers, prawns and cocktail sauce, something she could've done without, as far as I was concerned. I waited patiently for those tiny sausages in dough. She calls them pigs in a blanket. I could eat my weight in them. Instead, she said the brie cheese, ugh, was in the oven. Jake handed Hannah a tall ice-filled glass of bubbly liquid he called ginger ale. He, Patrick, and Izzie had short glasses of brown liquid from the bottle marked XXX Reserve.

Conversation centered around the early morning problem of Patrick's oil leak when the front door opened with a bang against the hall wall.

"Hello, everyone. Hope I've not missed anything. I could use a dry martini if there's a good bartender here." Olivia announced.

"Coming right up." Jake stood, hurried to the kitchen and reached for the Vermouth.

Olivia appeared fashionable in a heavy long black sweater with a cowl neckline. Leopard print leotards with black knee-length boots completed her look. She took a seat on the sectional, stretched her long legs in front of her and accepted the gin martini handed to her. I took a chance that she was in a good mood and jumped up beside her. I got an ear scratch.

"Izzie, the prawns are delicious, and your cocktail sauce is always the greatest." Olivia continued, "Jay couldn't come tonight. He got tied up with a project he's working on. He's so sorry."

"Oh, no, Mother," the sisters said in unison.

"So, he's not retired?" Izzie asked.

"No, dear." Olivia answered curtly. "Some people still need to work, but, oh my, he's such a dear. I've not been this happy since I was a teenager. It's too bad he couldn't make it, but he does have priorities that need attending to."

"We missed him at Thanksgiving and now again," sighed Hannah.

"He said he looked forward to getting to know everyone soon. I told him, 'that's okay'. We need to start making Christmas plans."

"Well, looks like we'll just have to wait till Christmas. At least we saw him at the Halloween party, so we know he's not a figment of Mother's imagination." Izzie said.

"Well, now we know his name," said Hannah. "You acted really happy at the masquerade party."

"I know, darlin'. I was. I am," She said with a hum. "So, tell me. What's the news here? Are you getting along with your therapist, Patrick? How's your beast of a dog doing?"

Well, at least Olivia and I agree on one thing. She said Nickie was a beast. I heard a tinge of criticism in her voice. Not from me. Nickie was becoming a good pal, not as great as Buddy, but still, a pal.

Patrick said, "My therapy is coming along, slowly, but I'm doing okay. I've started to use to a walker some around the house but still use the chair on outings. Nickie went for his first training today and did great, once we got there."

"What happened? Dogs can be like that. Did he balk and refuse to get in your car?"

"Quite the contrary. He hops right in behind the driver and sprawls out on the back seat."

"No, Olivia, it wasn't Nickie." Jake jumped into the conversation. "The problem was we discovered an oil leak caused by a loose nut to the oil pan filter. Lucky for us we noticed it before we took off for the kennels. We had to get one of Paul's service guys to come over. All in all, I'd say we had an eventful day from early morning until now. You've definitely brightened our day by your visit."

Olivia's tilted her head back and giggled as she gave Jake a wink and me a good ear scratch. Izzie turned away with a frown of what looked like disgust.

I'd always been aware Jake was one smooth talker. He proved it that night.

"Mother, you remember the stables in Germantown where I took riding lessons as a kid?" Hannah asked. "It's the same place. Still beautiful grounds, only the stalls have been turned into birthing areas for Black Russians Terriers."

Thank goodness Hannah talks distinctly. At one time, I thought one of the federal agents said there were terrorists living at the kennels.

Chapter 30

Patrick wore a brown hoodie the next morning when he and Nickie joined Izzie, Daisy, and me for our walk. He used his wheelchair, still not strong enough to handle Nickie, who sometimes lunged toward a blowing leaf. Izzie had just finished tying her running shoes and putting on our coats when he knocked.

Jake and Buddy left for the ranch at the break of sunlight after a mug of coffee and a bagel.

Patrick started our day by sharing a Nickie story. It seems Nickie had slid under their bed and wouldn't get out until Hannah coaxed him with some beef jerky. Patrick laughed when he said he was beginning to wonder if they would be raising two babies, Nickie and their little one. He hoped Nickie was better behaved by May.

We stepped off the elevator on the first floor to give Harry and Leona some brie from last night. Leona opened her front door and leaned forward to accept the cheese Izzie handed her.

"I was planning to call you today." Leona looked pretty in her lavender lounging set, her favorite color. "Yesterday Mr. Devore stopped by and asked if he could park his motorcycle in the vacant spot in the garage. It would be the empty spot next to your Mother's.

"He said it had a small leak, but he was getting it fixed soon. Until then, he had a catch-tray under it and rags to clean the floor if any dripped. I didn't think Olivia would care, do you? I told him I'd ask."

Why don't you ask me about the smell down here? It smells woody, like heavy leathery musk. I thought right then, The new guy wears Aramis.

Patrick's body stiffened and his lips curled at the word motorcycle. "They never found the SOB responsible for my accident." he muttered under his breath. He stayed in a gloomy mood the rest of the walk. After we returned, his mood began to change, he smiled as his watched us play in the courtyard.

I needed to hurry upstairs for some water, but Buddy had other plans. He and Nickie ran toward the oak tree, home of Mr. Squirrel. Leaves flew as the boys pounced and darted around the tree, having no more luck than before. With a sharp whistle Patrick summoned Nickie. Not familiar with the shrill sound, Buddy followed him back into the garage. Izzie unloaded the wheelchair from the hauling frame and helped Patrick situate himself. We headed for the elevator.

Miss Daisy and I allowed ourselves one more nature call, then hurried to catch Momma who entered the elevator as we approached. Upstairs, Nickie and Patrick went their way while we ran to our water bowls. Buddy with his usual sloppiness, created a mess on the floor for Momma to wipe up, or fall into.

I stood at our doorway to watch Momma walk across the hall. My sense of curiosity required I listen whenever she talked to Hannah.

"I'll be getting out the Christmas decorations today. I know you lost some of yours when your loft had the smoke and fire damage, so, if you want to come over, I can share."

"Thanks a million. I'd love to check-out your cast offs. Oh, rats. I just remembered. I have a doctor appointment at one."

"Want me to drive you?"

"That's sweet of you, but Patrick wants to go today. We're getting the info to help us decide whether we want a 4D Ultrasound before Christmas. He wants to wait, but I'm real eager to learn the sex so we can be prepared for him, or her.

"It's just as well. I'm working the night shift in the ER and could use a nap after lunch. Let's try for one day later this week, okay?"

"Sure." It was when Hannah turned to go into her apartment I noticed a bump on her front. I guessed a baby was really on its way.

Our earlier run had given me an appetite. I herded Daisy to come stand by me as I took a position in front of the refrigerator. All we had to do was stare at Izzie to let her know we were hungry. Momma knew some of our needs had been met through our walk and play. Our only request now was for food. She offered me a treat, but I refused. I was craving a boiled egg. My palate craved them more in the fall than any other time. I stood firm in front of the refrigerator with Daisy joining me in the stare game. It worked. She opened the refrigerator. Soon I heard a crack, meaning sweet Momma was peeling our eggs. My hunger would soon be replaced with a full, satisfied tummy.

Buddy slept through it all. After eating, we followed his example. I needed some peace and quiet. We snuggled in our circle and I drifted off. The mouse I'd seen skittered cross the kitchen floor this morning had outmaneuvered me again. I needed to dream up a plot to catch the little rascal.

Deep in my dog-think, or maybe in a dream, I was jolted to awareness by a bang, bang on the front door. Being a man of action, I bolted toward the sound as Izzie rounded the corner from the bedroom. Sweet Momma tripped over me. She caught herself on the bookcase in the hall, so there we were, grateful I hadn't hurt sweet Momma. I was shaken up by our near accident and not in any mood for guests, especially when Izzie opened the door to the federal agents.

To be truthful, I was upset to think they would come without calling.

I stood next to my Momma as she talked to them in the doorway. They asked to see Jake. She explained he would be back late that night. After some muffled, undistinguished talk, I concluded they would come back tomorrow at eleven in the morning. At that time, they wanted the conversation to include Patrick and Hannah. So much for a peaceful day. I had to dog-think about the reason those guys were back to annoy me. I completely forgot the mouse problem. More pressing issues needed my attention.

Izzie called Hannah about tomorrow's meeting, then set out clear plastic tubs containing shiny red ornaments and candles, tinsel and bells. She took a nap before going to her shift at St. Jude's. Our day was uneventful, sleeping most of the day until Hannah came over to take us downstairs for nature's call.

Nickie was with her. He sniffed and pawed at Buddy during the ride down, paying no attention to Daisy and me. The beast was in one of his playful, romping moods and enticed Buddy to chase him in the courtyard. Daisy and I were tempted to play but an evening north wind had chilled me to the bone. Daisy agreed. We stayed with Hannah after answering nature's call, then everyone headed toward the warmth of the elevator.

Suddenly, Hannah stopped. She hurried over to their SUV. With her hands on her hips, she slowly looked toward both back tires, then bent over and closely examined a back right one.

She called out to me, "Look Sammy, come here. Doesn't that back tire look low to you?" There she went again. Hannah forgets I can't respond to her. I could get disgusted with her, but instead I consider it a compliment she thinks I can answer.

I ran to her side, woofed for Nickie to follow. It was time to start teaching him his male duties. I showed him how I examined the tire, sniffed it and raised my leg. I liked to leave scent on every car tire I came upon. Nickie wagged his tail in excitement and did a grand job completing his lesson.

I admit, one of my earthly pleasures is to sniff and scent tires. Momma says 'no', but Hannah didn't seem to mind. She was right. I could see the long slit. I concluded, we definitely had a problem.

Chapter 31

Patrick rolled himself into the hallway when we got off the elevator. He took Nickie's leash from Hannah and herded his tired doggie home. Hannah led us toward our unit.

She opened our door to let us inside, then turned. "Patrick, I'm really frightened. I just found one of our back tires has been slashed. I didn't see anyone but, do you ever get the feeling someone is following you, especially in the garage? That gash wasn't an accident."

"No, sweetheart. I've never had the feeling I was being followed. Although I'm never alone down there. I'm usually talking to whomever is helping me load. No wonder you were frightened. I'll go make a police call now. You say, you didn't see anyone?"

"There's nothing I saw, just a feeling."

Our supper of kibble, pumpkin and liver tasted yummy. Buddy and I rushed to see who could clean our bowl first. I don't think he chewed a bite, just swallowed. He won. Daisy followed her same eating pattern.

Buddy snored loud and long before Jake got home in late evening. I knew from past experience my pal would not hear Jake, so I ran to greet him. Jake is the best ear scratcher ever. He uses both hands to get to that back place I cannot reach with my paw. He's also good for a treat if you greet him with a little yap.

It worked. I got one of those treats I go crazy for, salmon and sweet potato. A smackin' good treat. Izzie came home, early morning, and followed her after-work routine of oatmeal from the refrigerator and hot cocoa.

I'd watched her make her oatmeal concoction many evenings before going to work or to bed. She took a glass quart jar, filled it over half-way with raw oats, alternating unsweetened coconut, walnuts, and dried cranberries. Then she poured almond milk over the mixture and screwed on the lid. The next morning when she'd wake or come home from work, it was ready to eat. That day she ate it quickly, drank her cocoa and headed to bed for a nap.

Jake fed us our morning meal. We'd been to the courtyard and back before Izzie showed herself. Dressed in a bright red turtleneck and jeans she looked beautiful to this old dog. Her flawless olive skin was beautiful even without make-up. She pranced around the kitchen, hummed Christmas carols, and gave Jake a firm kiss. We dogs got a loving pat. All this and she didn't spill the OJ. I loved her more than a tasty steak. Watching her made my tail go tap, tap, tap with happiness.

After several cuckoos, Patrick and Hannah came over. Nickie stayed beside Patrick's wheelchair for a couple minutes, then ran into the kitchen. I knew he'd spied my arch nemesis because he growled as he pawed the pantry door. Nickie's pawing rattled the door so powerfully I thought it might pop off its hinges. Finally, without success, he gave up, sprawled under the coffee table and fell to sleep.

I trotted over to Nickie. He needed to be set straight on a few things. It was my responsibility to take charge of his education. As I watched him, I realized it would take several dog-talk sessions to teach that pup who was the alpha dog. I woofed at him. He turned to me, starred with his jet-black eyes and stood to an amazing height. To my mind, he'd grown two inches overnight.

I looked up and explained he must never run off to chase a mouse even though he might think his master was settled. He should stay close to appraise any new environment. Nickie wagged his black curly tail during my instruction. His friendly action let me know he was an eager student.

As the cuckoo sang several notes, there was a knock on the front door. Izzie went to answer. I trotted close behind. Sure enough, there stood Mr. Grey and Mr. Blue Suits, the federal agents.

After the formality of offering tea, which was refused, Grey Suit snorted and began. "It has been called to our attention, some of you are going to the BRT kennel. At first we questioned whether you were going to participate in the illegal gambling or to look at the dogs. Now, I see your BRT under the coffee table. Perhaps, my question is answered."

Blue Suit asked, "We need to know to what extent you have participated in the gambling. What have you observed? What were the names of the players?"

"Before I answer your questions, I have one for you." Patrick said. "Why have you been following me, what are you looking for? There is no reason for your surveillance of me. I'm a professor and have nothing to hide."

Blue Suit scrunched his eyebrows and looked puzzled hearing the questions. "We're sorry to have alarmed you, sir. I'll answer your questions momentarily. We explained to Ms. DeLisle nearly two months ago we were conducting a criminal inquiry regarding active illegal gaming headed by a notorious criminal, Mr. Abram Cohen.

We were investigating a violation of the IRS tax code. That means when we discovered avoidance of tax payments, we started an investigation. This relates to high stake Texas Hold'em games and perhaps money laundering under the guise of the sale of expensive Black Russians, selling for twenty-five to forty-thousand dollars."

Those men got me so confused. I finally realized they meant to say the dogs were high priced, not the Russian people. I jumped on the sofa beside Izzie and snuggled between her hip and the arm of the chair, laying my head on her leg. Buddy was across the room by Jake on full alert, watching the men with unwavering interest. Daisy had no idea the seriousness of this meeting and chased the yellow/green squeeze ball around the kitchen floor. Nickie snored, still under the coffee table.

"It's unfortunate," Grey Suit said, "for all concerned, Mr. Cohen was murdered before we could conclude the investigation. Had he been found guilty of this violation, he would have been subject to substantial penalties and criminal charges. Based on information from local authorities, we have concluded his death is related to these activities in some form yet to be determined."

Blue Suit continued the conversation. "This is where we believe your uncle Jessie DeLisle enters the picture. We know from a Memphis surgeon that Avi Greenbucks, also known as Abram Cohen, brought Jessie to this surgeon for reconstructive surgery."

He turned in his chair toward Hannah. "In our endeavor to tie this complimented scene together, we came to know the word 'Uncle' is not the correct word you would use for Jessie DeLisle, Miss Hannah. Is that correct?"

Hannah gasped, her hands flew to her belly. She stiffened, bit her lower lip and frowned, tears running down her blushed face. "How dare you bring up such a personal matter," she shrieked at them.

"Madam, we mean you no disrespect. As we probed into Mr. Cohen's life, we learned the connection between he and Mr. DeLisle could be traced back to when they were young, their middle twenties.

"It also came to surface that the man you'd grown up thinking was your uncle was really your father. Your mother and he had been lovers before she married his brother. This had been kept from you until two years ago, about the time of the cruiser explosion. Isn't that true?"

"Yes, you're correct," Hannah's lower lip quivered.

"In fact, we want to help you, or at least, your husband." Blue Suit leaned forward looking directly at Patrick. "Professor, we were following you, not that we suspected any wrong-doing on your part, but only to protect you. There is a strong possibility the accident you suffered was an attempted homicide."

Hannah slumped sideways and fell against Patrick.

"She's fainted," Izzie yelled.

Chapter 32

Izzie brought smelling salts while Patrick applied a cool cloth to the forehead of his pregnant wife. She lay on the sectional, covering her eyes with her hands.

"You should know." Patrick said, "I've been witness to some strange out of the ordinary occurrences lately. Also, my wife at times has had an uneasy feeling she was being watched. Was that your man?"

Grey Suit asked, "No, we did not have any surveillance on your wife. Can you clarify your strange experiences, please?"

"Lately, I'd say since I've returned from the hospital and rehab center, I've witnessed some unusual incidents. Jake was with me the day the oil pan was leaking due to an unscrewed nut on it. About three days later while attempting to attach my wheelchair to the rack on the back of the SUV, the rack came loose and fell to one side. Had I not paid attention, I would've been thrown from the chair. At that time, I additionally noticed the three straps for attaching the chair had been cut and the ratchets dislodged.

"I called the garage who had installed the wheelchair device. They came, tightened the bolts, repaired the straps and checked it out. I never told Hannah or anyone about it. Although highly unlikely, maybe the nut of the oil pan could have worked loose but not the lug nuts of the chair rack. It would've taken a strong person to loosen them."

"So, you didn't you tell anyone?"

"No, I was getting stronger and vowed to be on the lookout for problems. Then, yesterday when Hannah walked the dogs she came back to tell me a tire had been slit. This was one of the times she felt someone was watching her. She had the dogs, so she wasn't scared anyone would try to hurt her. But, you can imagine, she had cause for alarm. Slitting the tire was no accident. Therefore, it appears that you are on the right track, whatever track it is."

Izzie interrupted with a commanding voice. "You're possibly on the right track, but I think the motive is different. Maybe Uncle Jessie, Hannah's father, isn't wanting to hurt Patrick as much as he is wanting to protect Hannah. Two years ago, this Christmas, Patrick and Hannah were married. Yet, we heard nothing from Jessie.

"Why? Perhaps because he was recuperating from surgery. I believe he wanted to prevent that marriage, thinking in his depraved brain, that Patrick would harm Hannah like Patrick's grandmother, Clarabelle, had harmed him. I do know he was determined to find her letter to Hannah and me. I still have it, hidden away."

Patrick added, "Growing up, as children we were always conscious of how protective Jessie was of Hannah, whom we thought at that time, was his niece. Maybe he was actually showing his genuine love for a daughter he could only love under the guise of being her uncle."

"Mother always found it hard to believe he had anything to do with causing the explosion of the cruiser because he was a different person with her and us girls, caring and kind," said Izzie. "This foolish idea of hers is part of the riff between me and my mother. She insists he didn't intentionally do it, the gas line had a leak. I was there. I know he did."

Grey Suit exchanged a glance with Blue Suit. "I'm not sure where we're going with this conversation. We'd like to come back tomorrow.

It might help us if you could have the letter you've referred to available. Same time?"

Both stood and walked toward the door. Hannah listened to Izzie's theory without comment, then stood and pushed Patrick's chair. She stopped for a second, sighed as she turned to the agents, "Will we have to give up our loft?"

"No, Madam," Blue Suit answered. "Mr. Cohen bought it from your father nearly thirty years ago, long before this investigation."

Buddy and Jake followed everyone to the door. Jake shut the door, uttered a loud sigh and walked toward Izzie with outstretched arms.

I had to take a moment to do some serious dog-thinking. Hannah and Patrick may keep their home, but I have a grim feeling Miss Princess my not be an heiress for very long.

Chapter 33

We finished our supper of kibble, asparagus pieces with bites of steak on top. Buddy, who always finished eating first, rolled around on his back under the coffee table stretching his legs straight up in the air. Disgusting. The sun crept behind the Mississippi as Hannah appeared. She explained after her long nap she was more relaxed. She needed a distraction and was ready to help Izzie decorate their lofts for the Christmas season. She appeared calm as she helped Momma open the storage tubs.

"Patrick just unpacked our nativity set," Hannah said, "the one he's had since he was a boy. Through many Christmas-messes, rain and thunderstorms he's kept all the figures unharmed. We've used them every year. After he gets the figures and manger assembled to set up outside, he'll be over to rehash this morning's conversation."

Hannah hummed *White Christmas* as she sat on the floor and unwrapped candles while Izzie, in the kitchen, stirred her marinara sauce. Since my puppy days, I've known the smell of garlic, onion and tomatoes meant Momma was making spaghetti sauce or chili. I like the beef Momma fries to put in the sauce. She always hands me little tidbits if I beg. This is the only food I beg for. I can't help it. The smell is just much too powerful to let me stay seated. Standing on my bottom, my front paws waved in excitement. Sweet Momma responded with bites. Daisy joined me today. We happily licked our lips as we enjoyed the treat.

Momma laughed. Then, I saw the mouse. There he was in plain view, taunting me to go after him. Although tempted, I thought it wasn't the time to distract Momma. Daisy missed seeing him. Buddy was sleeping, so we ate our meat treat and laid down in our beds.

The door opened with a bang. Patrick was red faced as he rolled into the living room. The odd thing was Nickie, who stood beside him, looked like he had a large odd-shaped ball in his mouth.

"This dog will not make it to adulthood if he keeps this up," Patrick shouted as he rolled his chair over by the windows. "Can someone grab that dog?"

Nickie, in his happy, puppy mood ran around the loft holding his ball in his mouth. Hannah looked up and pushed herself forward and started after him. Izzie motioned Hannah to set back and she took up the pursuit. Now Buddy joined in the fun. For some reason, perhaps my super instinct, I stayed in bed with Daisy. Down the hall and back again they ran.

Jake stepped in front of the runners and yelled "Nickie, Stop. Treat."

That did it. Let me tell you, that black beast can stop on a dime if he wants. Only then did I see Nickie had the head of one of the Three Wise Men in his mouth.

I had a good laugh and let me say, for the record, "That wise man will be winking the rest of his life." The sisters winked at each other and tried to hide a giggle. Patrick held the face of Nickie in his hands and said some words that sounded to me like a scolding mixed with laughter.

Sweet Momma and Hannah hummed carols as they strung lights and hung wreaths throughout the loft. The girls filled two containers with decorations to go home with Hannah. Jake carried them over. I got in the holiday mood by tapping my tail, one of my happiest expressions, in unison with one of their carols.

Jin-gle Bells, Tap, Tap. Tap.

Chapter 34

T
he next day, the knock came as cuckoo bird sang eleven. Those eleven o'clock visits were beginning to seem routine. As Izzie's closest companion I trotted close to her heels when she went to answer the door. Blue Suit was coming around. On that particular day he brought four chewy bone treats, two small and two large. Buddy and Nickie devoured theirs in three gulps. Daisy and I, being more refined eaters, ate a couple bites, then went to our selected areas to hide the rest of ours for later.

The agents were more relaxed on that visit, greeted Patrick and Hannah who had come by earlier. Everyone opted for cups of Jake's finest roast. Jake explained the roasting procedure as he prepared them coffee using a French press. When I first heard Jake and Izzie talk about a French press, still a puppy at the time, I thought it odd they pressed their clothes with coffee beans. Humans do get their words mixed up. Dog-speak is much easier to understand.

Each agent smiled and nodded their head in approval as they tasted the hot liquid, then walked back to the living room carrying their steaming mugs. We canines seated ourselves comfortably beside our family members.

I jumped up beside Izzie in her favorite green lounge chair, Daisy followed and tried her best to push between us. No luck. I tolerated her more than when she first came to live with us, but no one, I mean, no one, gets between me and my Momma. On second thought, Jake might be an exception to that statement.

Everyone was seated, or standing, as was the case of Nickie who chose to lean against Patrick's chair. Buddy lay at Jake's feet, his head resting on his human's shoe.

Hannah leaned back on the sectional and adjusted the cushions against her back.

"Before we begin with our report," Grey Suit said, "you need to know local authorities have reported a rash of burglaries. These took place about six months ago. It's believed the last two robberies, occurring at *Mednikow Jewelers* here in Memphis, may have some connection in this case. Keeping this information in mind, the Department has evaluated the information and arrived at these conclusions.

"It is now established, after the explosion of your cruiser two years ago, your uncle-father, Jessie DeLisle, sought the assistance of Mr. Abram Cohen, a longtime acquaintance. With the help of Cohen, he was able to change his appearance. His makeover, which took over a year to heal, covered the time of your wedding, Hannah. With his new falsified records, he was able to change his complete identity.

"These personal identification records were obtained through Mr. Cohen's lawyer. We believe there was a huge debt created because of Mr. Cohen's support. Mr. DeLisle was employed to work for his friend to pay off this debt.

"Are you saying Uncle Jessie was working for Mr. Cohen all this time?" Izzie tugged on my ears.

"Oh, yes. Due to the amount of trust between the two, his employment put Mr. DeLisle in control of gambling operations owned by Cohen. The operation ran out of what had once been a horse facility in Germantown. The stables owned by members of the Wilson family, sold the buildings and acreage to Cohen approximately ten year ago.

He converted the structures from horse stables to deluxe dog kennels, naming the facility the *BRT Holiday Kennels*, i.e. Black Russian Terrier Holiday Kennels.

"Dogs of this breed, as you undoubtedly know, are highly prized for their intelligence, strength, and devotion making them a masterful guard and service animal. These dogs sold as puppies for twenty-five thousand dollars, trained service and guard dogs for up to forty thousand dollars."

Blue Suit took a sip of his steaming coffee. "During that period of time, the Bureau was investigating Mr. Cohen under the IRS code for unpaid taxes. Understand, we were not looking for Mr. DeLisle. Local authorities had his information in a dead file. The facts that brought him under surveillance were due to his association with Abram Cohen."

Jake sat his coffee mug on the table to his left. "So, you're saying you did not know the two cases were intertwined when you started the investigation?"

"Right." Blue Suit answered. "Although Cohen seemed to lead a simple life, he actually ran a state-wide operation of crime and corruption. We believe several jewelry store burglaries and robberies can also be attributed to his mandate. The loss was high and included loose cut diamonds, expensive rings, and pendants as well as cash. He dictated all actions undertaken by his men here and in Florida."

I snuggled against Momma. She stroked my back in long strokes while I stayed awake and listened. I glanced at Daisy to see her head nod and her eye lids flutter, then close. I wasn't sure if Daisy took in any of the information about her beloved human. If she understood he was a crook, she seemed unbothered by the news. Knowing the Princess, her lack of interest was to be expected.

Buddy, like me, was alert, ears on point. Nickie had joined Buddy with, I'm happy to say, notable curiosity in regard to the conversation. I gave him a stern look, reminding him to pay attention and not be glancing toward the kitchen.

"Surveillance of Cohen at this building," Blue Suit continued, "and at his place in Florida starting last summer, began to reveal a change in his actions. A much different picture began to emerge. These were the weeks when you, Miss Izzie, were spending time in Nesbit, Mississippi. A gentleman we didn't recognize began making routine visits to this building. They flew together one weekend to Florida. Through the information gathered by our confidential informant we learned this person of interest was visiting unit 4-B. During this period, we could find no facial recognition of this person in our system."

Grey Suit interrupted. "During the time of these visits, several substantial burglaries took place within the state of Tennessee, noticeably two large robberies at local jewelers. These robberies broadened Cohen's area of crime. They were, for lack of a better classification, new endeavors. Conversation overheard between Cohen and the unidentified man at Larry's bar revealed an argument concerning the split of the take which we now believe lead to the murder of Cohen.

"We now believe the unidentified man to be Jessie DeLisle. All activity in the unit had ceased two days before your return, leading us up to the time when you, Miss DeLisle, discovered the body."

Daisy raised her head, looked around, stretched, did her back-leg flutter kick and went back to sleep. Nickie nudged closer to Patrick's chair and watched, perhaps a little too possessively, as Patrick rubbed Hannah's back. Later I woofed him not to be jealous.

"After an interview with a local plastic surgeon," Grey Suit continued, "we know Jessie to be the man who came here during the week leading up to the robberies. Cameras provided at the two local robberies lead us to believe Jessie was the leader, perhaps, along with Cohen, who was the mastermind of these robberies. Three persons were picked up on street surveillance leaving the scene of the robbery. Neither the one round faced, perhaps bald, overweight man could be Jessie nor the other, toting a reddish beard. These are out of the question. But, the third man—"

Whoa. Wait a minute. I sat up and let out couple barks. They just described the guys I saw at the memorial service and again at the poker table. I barked again. Why didn't Jake or Patrick speak up. Listen, guys, this is important. Tell them. I barked again. Nothing.

Izzie turned to me "Hush, Sammy. These men are talking."

Darn, I know that. I'm trying to tell you all, I've seen them. That was one of the very few occasions when I wished I could human speak.

Chapter 35

There was no way to stop this conversation. I was in a quandary about what to do next. Buddy's glance my way let me know he understood my dilemma. Like I've said before, Buddy is fast on the uptake of clues. We'd never seen anything like this on our Perry Mason reruns. 'Better to hush and listen' was the message he'd sent me. So, I hushed and tried to listen.

"Jessie DeLisle is now believed to be our lead into Cohen's illegal activities. He was the one person Cohen trusted. Yet, he may be the one —unlikely but possibly—who murdered Cohen. I'll say, we have a lot of questions for him when we find him."

Blue Suit took another sip. "We have been unable to locate Jessie's whereabouts, or where he hangs out. He might be living at the kennels or anywhere. We know he drives a Harley. He got away twice when we were tailing him. He moved in and out of traffic like a professional driver.

"This brings us to our concern regarding you, Professor Guffin. It is our belief, for whatever reason, the suspected person, Jessie DeLisle, alias Jerry Devilin is trying to kill you."

Grey Suit turned to Izzie. "Would someone read the letter you believe may be at the root of these problems?"

Izzie stroked the nape of her neck. She frowned as she turned to the table beside her. She reached for, picked up, then laid a manila envelope in her lap. She slid a stained piece of paper carefully from the envelope and began to read.

April 2, 1983

My name is Clarabelle Guffin, wife of Mac Guffin. I write this for my girls, Hannah and Izzie 'bout their daddy and what I saw. Tho I call you my girls, I knows you're not my birth babies, but I love you just as if you are.

I haft to write what I saw yesterday before I forget, tho I'll never forget that horrible sight. I knows I won't be believed cause of who I am, but I knows what I saw so I put it on this paper just so someday my darlin's will know the truth.

Yesterday I's going to the library taken Mr. Matt and Izzie some ginger snaps. I heard a pop, pop. Going round the corner into the hallway I's heard 'nother, same sound. It's then I seen dis man run out the library room and out da back door.

I's only seen the side of his face coming out the door, but I seen nough to know him. Anyways I know that buckskin jacket. As I stared, the sun lit on his cock belt buckle. Then I knows for sure I seen Mr. Jessie. As God is my witness and on my blessed momma's grave, I seen Mr. Jessie, your daddy's brother, run from that room.

Oh, Lordy, the mess in that room I'll never forget. Mr. Matt, out of his wheelchair, on the floor in a pool of blood, blood all over de place. Precious Izzie on the floor. Little puppy Stella whimpering behind the sofa.

I don't know who called who cause I was holdin' little Izzie in my arms. People were all around. Since I'd heard two pops I's sure you were shot too. I was scared I'd lost you.

Someone says you were passed out, then in a coma. You've never woke up all night. Miss Olivia and I were with you till early this mornin' when those doctors sent us home. He said it could take a long time for you to come round but I's going back after I get things settled here. Your Momma's got all them funeral things to take care of. I'll not leave you tills you wake, no matter how long it takes. Poor Hannah, you all scared and confused but yo Momma will see no harm comes to you while sister Izzie in in the hospital..

My heart aches for your loss. Mr. Matt was feared by some, but I saw the sadness many times in his eyes. He was a kind and generous man to me and my family, and he loved you sweet things as good or better than any daddy I knows.

God bless you sweet darlins. Yo knows I write this from my love for you. I holds you close in my heart till my dyin' day and beyond.

Your true and faithful friend, Clarabelle

Izzie sat quietly. Clarabelle's letter lay in her lap. Hannah sobbed softly as she leaned back into the cushions of the sectional. Not a word was spoken by anyone. I licked Izzie's hand. Buddy and Daisy snored. Nickie licked Patrick's hand to give him comfort.

"Oh, shit," said Patrick. "Are you telling me those incidents really were planned? No wonder Jessie, or whatever he calls himself, wants that letter. I'd forgotten how powerful it is. I'm so ashamed. A careless mechanic wasn't to blame when he installed the wheelchair rack. Jessie probably cut those straps. I took that poor guy over the coals. Never suspected anything else."

"This is why the Bureau would like to enlist your service."

Chapter 36

That afternoon I spent in something like a zombie zone. I could not believe the Jessie in the letter could be the one who had again murdered. Murdered the well-liked Mr. Cohen. The neighbor we all thought was kindhearted and gentle. I was puzzled that I didn't judge Mr. Cohen correctly.

"When I think of the number of conversations I've had with Mr. Cohen, thinking him an elderly, charming man, I'm in disbelief he was a notorious crook," Izzie said.

"I agree," said Jake. "He was soft spoken and pleasant, not someone I would imagine as the leader of a crime syndicate."

Buddy and I did serious dog-think. We went back to the topic regarding the men described by the agents I'd seen at the kennels. He came up with a great idea regarding the clues we'd hidden in the laundry room. We would show the oily rag and poker chips when the need arose.

Before two that afternoon, Hannah and Patrick left for their visit with the obstetrician. Hannah was excited when she dropped Nickie off with us. I wasn't at all surprised to see the wise man's head carried in by Nickie like a prize trophy.

"We can't wait to hear what the ultrasound shows. We'll stop by Kroger to get salad fixins' to go with the pasta," she said.

"Remember a loaf of French bread," Izzie yelled to her sister,

You'll never believe what I'm about to tell you happened four cuckoos later.

The front door opened. Patrick and Hannah rushed in, actually Hannah rushed, Patrick, using his walker, was much slower. Hannah plopped a Kroger bag on the kitchen cabinet and yelled, "Babies. Two of them. We can't believe it. Twins. We're having twin boys."

Izzie turned from the kitchen sink with dripping wet hands and grabbed her sister in a tight embrace. Jake stood from the kitchen table and shook Patrick's hand. A lot of talking at the same time followed.

"Forget the supper for now. Open the wine to celebrate. Oh, sorry, Hannah. I forgot you shouldn't drink." said Izzie.

"Hey, sis, just this once, one tiny glass. Add an ice cube to melt and weaken it," said Hannah. "A toast to our growing families."

Glasses tapped all around.

"I can tell you all, I nearly fainted when several arms and legs started showing on the screen. It didn't register what we were seeing."

"Then," chimed in Patrick, "two tiny penises appeared, and we knew, two boys. We need to start getting the nursery ready while Hannah is still able to be up."

Hannah added, "The doctor explained its common for twins to come at least one month early."

Patrick grabbed Hannah's hand and kissed it. "That's after a two month or more bed rest. She's got about six weeks before the complete bed rest starts. Looks like I've got time to intensify my physical therapy. I'll be using my walker just in time to take care of my gal."

What about the black beast? I wondered but barked not a word. It's possible the little ones will think they have a pony in their house. What a great babysitter he'll be. Well, on second thought, time will tell on that brainwave.

Before the pasta was served, Izzie fed us our kibble without dropping a single nugget. A lot of happy baby talk followed as they ate. It was of no interest to us. We went to our doggie beds. Daisy tried to get into mine. She sleeps with me sometimes because her bed is so lumpy. I will not sleep in it even if she woofs me to come on over. It crinkles when I try to get comfortable. Not for me, I choose my bed or Momma's to get my rest.

"Shall we set up the tree?" Izzie asked.

"We'd better go home. I'm bushed," said Hannah.

"She's right. It has been a one-of-a-kind day. Thanks for a great Italian dinner." said Patrick as he rolled his chair toward the door. Nickie rose, stretched doing his downward dog and followed with the Wise Man's head held securely in his mouth. I do believe Nickie won the battle of the Wise Man.

While Sweet Momma loaded the dishwasher, Jake brought the tree box from the storage room, untied the box and began to take out branches. Izzie, hands on her hips, watched, then said, "Shouldn't we move the furniture in place before going any further? We need to be able to place the tree in front of the glass wall."

"Right, you are, sweetheart. Let's move the dog beds over to the side of the room and flip the sectional around to the left." He grabbed Buddy's bed and walked across the living room.

Izzie bent over, picked up my bed, set it on Daisy's and stood. "Wow, Daisy's bed is heavy. Can you check this out? It's at least five pounds more than his even though they 're the same size,"

She dropped mine to the floor and set Daisy's on the sectional for a better look. Daisy and I were under foot as Izzie called it, but I was curious to see what she was referring to.

"Man, you're right. Her bed is sure heavy compared to the others. I guess we didn't notice when we brought it over because so many of her things were stacked on it. Look, this end has been sewed closed by hand."

"Go ahead and remove the cover. I probably need to wash all the bed covers anyway." And then Izzie gathered some pillows in her arms.

Jake pulled the tan threads from the fuzzy fabric. Inside, between two layers of foam were some clear plastic bags. Jake pulled more threads to make the opening larger, then yelled, "Izzie, look, get a load of this."

"What? What is it?"

Jake pulled out a clear plastic bag. Inside were several purple velvet bags. He sat on the sectional and pulled the draw string on one of the bags. Into his hand fell several shiny rocks, many the size of kibble, some larger, a few smaller.

Izzie sat beside him. "They look like uncut diamonds. There's more. Get a load of this bag, diamond rings and a couple broaches.

Jake, do you remember the Suits talking about the jewelry heists? They thought Mr. Cohen was the mastermind behind them? If these prove to be from those robberies, these items will prove their suspicions were right on," Izzie said.

"There's more." Jake said as he pulled out some green bills, wrapped with a narrow white piece of paper. "These are one hundred-dollar bills wrapped in two thousand-dollar bundles."

"Are you sure?"

"You're darn tootin'." Jake answered. "There must be forty thousand here."

Izzie flopped back on the sofa. "No wonder his loft was ransacked. There was more than a struggle. Someone was looking for this stash."

Jake went to the kitchen and reached for the XXX Reserve bottle.

"After the intruder trashed the place searching for the loot, imagine we found it in Daisy's bed. Clever man, that Cohen."

"Maybe not too clever, he's dead," said Izzie.

Daisy heard her name and came running to Izzie. Buddy and I did our little dog laughs. I thought about the rag and poker chips we found in that bloody bathroom. I yapped and looked at Buddy. He woofed back, "no". He has a great sense of timing. I did nothing but wag my tail and listen.

I listened carefully as Momma carried some of the bags to the kitchen. "Grab the rest of the loot and help me."

"Help you do what?

"Pull out the refrigerator," said Momma. "See those six bricks waist high? Take them out. Daddy had a safe built in the wall. We'll put all this in there until the agents come tomorrow."

My Sweet Momma is sure one smart cookie.

Chapter 37

Mr. Cuckoo left his house on the kitchen wall and sang seven morning cuckoos as Izzie sliced the bagels on the granite countertop. She dropped them in the toaster, then retrieved the butter and purple jam from the refrigerator. Momma wore her customary Keds, jeans and, today, a teal turtleneck. Her auburn hair was tied in a ponytail. I loved to watch it sway back and forth in a swish, swish as she turned from the cabinet to the sink.

Jake grabbed a buttered bagel, attached our leashes and rushed us on our morning walk to answer nature's call. I didn't care. I was chilled to my bones as pellets of sleet filled the air and landed on my red parka. We wasted no time. We hadn't seen any bushy tailed critters in weeks. Buddy woofed he thought Mr. Squirrel was scared to come out. I thought he was getting his winter rest. If Nickie and Daisy had any thoughts on the subject, they didn't share them.

As he hurried us on to the gliding room, Jake said he needed to help Momma straighten the mess they had made last night during the tree decorating. Hannah and Patrick were going to our loft as we hopped off the elevator, happy to be in our warm home. They had no idea the news they were about to hear.

The Suits would be arriving at eleven o'clock, their given hour. Buddy and I woofed about how shocked they would be when Jake showed the treasures, or maybe I should say, loot, found in Daisy's bed.

After loading the dishwasher, Sweet Momma fashioned a green, red, and white antique quilt around the trunk of the fake tree. I'm the reason they used a fake one. You see, when I was a very young pup, I found the fresh tree intoxicating to my grand sniffing ability. It smelled so good, so, of course, I needed to leave my mark. When Momma took down the tree that first year, she remarked the tree had a bad odor around the trunk. The second year she saw me welcome it with a good sniff and my personal spray. We've had a fake tree ever since. So much for the real things in life.

Like clockwork, on the eleventh cuckoo, the Suits arrived. Blue Suit reached down in his navy wool jacket and handed the four of us a treat. While Izzie made hot cocoa for herself and Hannah, Jake prepared the French press coffee for the guys.

My nose twitched at the morning blend of a hint of citrus and rich chocolate. I spun around in circles, my happy tail went Tap, Tap, Tap and I don't even drink coffee. The Suits went to the kitchen to be served fresh brewed coffee, then carried their steaming hot mugs to the living room.

Izzie began by telling everyone how she and Jake where moving the dog beds to set up the Christmas tree. I could tell she took much too much time to tell her story. Grey Suit frowned with an annoyed look and rolled his eyes as he squirmed in his chair. When she finished, Jake appeared from the kitchen. Grey Suit's expression changed as he watched what happened next.

Jake displayed the plastic bags, spread them on the coffee table, revealing the cash and numerous purple velvet bags. Talk about a snort when Grey Suit gasped.

Grey and Blue Suit each picked up a purple bag. As they opened the draw strings some of the contents fell through their fingers and on the floor. The Agents sat, wide-eyed and speechless. Each reached for the diamonds on the floor, bumping their heads as they leaned forward. They straightened as Blue Suit pumped his fist in the air, perhaps feeling triumphant they had been right in their assumptions.

It appeared by the size of this find, Mr. Cohen had not divided the spoils of the robbery but had kept this much for himself. I'd be mad too if I stole a bunch of treats then my partner kept them. Of course, I'd know better than to do such a thing in the first place. Mr. Cohen would still be alive if he's followed my way of doing business.

Buddy looked at me, his ears up, on alert. I got the signal. While the adults in the group looked at the jewelry and money, off we scurried to retrieve the hidden items we had salvaged from Mr. Cohen's loft.

I trailed Buddy as we left the storeroom where our items had been safely hidden behind Jake's burlap bag of coffee beans. He had the two poker chips in his mouth. The oily rag, a companion to the one stuffed in Mr. Cohen's mouth, I drug behind me. I had a distinct dislike for the taste of oil, but we needed to present our clues.

Buddy made the decision to drop his chips in front of Grey Suit. I trotted around the coffee table, over to Blue Suit, my favorite of the two agents. I tugged the oily rag over his right shoe and stepped back wagging my tail in satisfaction for what I had delivered. Praise came my way from Blue Suit. "You're a good boy. What have you brought me, Little Guy?"

"Looks like I've got poker chips," said Grey Suit. "Why?"

Izzie, unable to sit still, stood, rubbing her hands together. She licked her lips as she spoke. "I know why. Remember, when I found Mr. Cohen in the bloody bathtub? There was a rag stuffed in his mouth along with a poker chip. When the cops got there, those items were gone. These guys are telling us these were left behind."

"They probably found them before the police came. The poker chip could be evidence. It's clear there could be fingerprints on these items, particularly the chip."

Buddy and I exchanged glances. I knew Perry Mason would be proud we'd used the training we received watching his reruns. This confirmed we had the noses required to be great detectives.

"Perhaps there will be some prints of these bags. We'll have all these items ran through forensics, checked for prints and DNA as soon as we get to the office.

"The purpose of this visit," Grey Suit raised his eyebrows and continued, "initially was to enlist the help of Patrick and Jake in connection with the case we are conducting. Now it could include much more. This file now includes the investigation of the criminal activities of the deceased Abram Cohen and a set of circumstances regarding Jessie DeLisle."

Chapter 38

I sniffed a sense of calm, of satisfaction in the air after that visit. A scheme had been devised to gain inside information from the gamblers about Mr. Cohen's activities and murder. During these conversations, the agents hoped they would learn the whereabouts of Uncle Jessie, alias Jerry Devilin, now a person in interest in the criminal case.

The agents came up with a plan which they drew out on the coffee table. After a lot of talking, nodding of heads, the men shook hands agreeing on a blueprint for their action. Mr. Grey Suit tilted his head and snorted slightly as he explained a commercial paneled truck would be close by to record everything said in the poker house.

The plan was for Jake to wear the wire. He would be with the gamblers much longer. Patrick would be training some of the time with Nickie at the center. Both he and Patrick would be paid as undercover informants. The Bureau would advance five thousand dollars to cover their gambling expenses. In exchange, Patrick would continue to use his wheelchair while there for Nickie's training each Wednesday and Friday. Jake, as his driver, would naturally be with him for each session and pass his time at the gaming table. These were the days Nickie was scheduled for his service dog sessions.

Only four more training sessions were scheduled before Patrick started his work outs with Nickie, so time was limited as to how long he and Jake would be included in the games. The guys would follow their same routine, take Nickie for his lesson, play some Texas-Hold'em and encourage the players to talk. It was easy for a guy like me to go along. I always hopped in the car and quietly followed Jake. I was a smart, low-key detective, having been taught by the best, Perry Mason. Tomorrow would be Wednesday, a game day.

While their strategy was being laid out, Momma sat in her longue chair She told me she was reading a Mr. Hemmingway. She added nothing to their conversation, but I know my Momma. I can tell her uneasiness, her apprehension, sometimes by the way she massages her temples or by the way her eyes narrow when she glances sideways. She glanced sideways a lot as she read. I knew my Momma had a plan of her own.

A boring day for me. No one wanted to play. Nothing to do but scratch my belly and listen.

Chapter 39

I awoke the next morning to the sound of Momma's phone ringing. After a few downward dogs, I trotted into the kitchen to see Jake and Izzie, holding hands, spinning around and laughing like little kids. Izzie saw me, stopped, and reached down to give my ears a scratch. She said, "Sammy, you're the first to know. My doctor just called with wonderful news. You are getting a brother or sister next fall."

I looked straight into my Sweet Momma's eyes and turned my head slightly to the right to hear her better. What did I hear? Maybe I was still asleep. Another dog in house? Thank goodness it wouldn't be a cat. Wait, on second thought, maybe a cat could help me catch that darn mouse in the pantry. I turned around, ran as fast as I could to my toy box and dug among my toys until I found my favorite, my green turtle. I ran back to Momma and dropped it at her feet.

"Oh, my dear boy. You thought I meant another doggie. No, my little love sponge, I meant a real baby. Our own baby, to grow up with its cousins, Hannah's boys."

Oh, wow. At that moment, Buddy came around the corner, did his downward dog and hurried over to me. Hey, Buddy, wait until you hear this. We've just got Daisy trained, now we must take on a new one, a real baby human. One of those humans that cries a lot.

We'll be free until fall, Buddy woofed. Ever the optimist, I let it go. Daisy sighed and walked toward her food bowl, having no idea of the work we faced in the coming months.

About mid-morning Izzie called Hannah to ask if she and Patrick were free on Saturday evening. She wanted them, Olivia and her friend for dinner. Maybe she and Jake were going to make an announcement. I never found out because of the turn of events that unfortunately followed.

Jake and I listened on speaker phone when Izzie called her mother to extend the invitation.

"We'd love to come. We are really looking forward to having a pre-holiday visit. My life has taken a different turn and I want to share it with you girls. I know you'll accept my decision when I explain my reason. Can we draw names like we did last year for presents?"

"Sure, Mother. That's a grand idea. Shall the limit be one hundred fifty since we're only buying one gift each? Do you want to include Jay in the gift giving?"

"Sounds good to me. Speaking of Jay and presents. Have I got a surprise for you girls?" Olivia said. "Yesterday I got my Christmas present from Jay. He said he couldn't wait until Christmas, so he gave it to me early."

"You sound so excited. What in the world is it?" Izzie said.

"Well, I declare, it'll knock your eyes out," Olivia answered. "It's a three-caret emerald cut diamond set in platinum. Thin tapered baguettes on either side make it a bewitching setting."

My Momma was so quiet I think I heard the mouse sneeze. Wow. Did this mean what I thought it might? Who had given her the ring? Who really was this Jay guy?

Buddy and I were sharing our thoughts when I heard Jake say it was time to 'GO' to the kennel. I wasted no time in following him into the hall, down the elevator with Nickie and Patrick. Patrick, usually keen on showing his progress with his walker, decided to follow the agent's suggestion. The instructions required he use the wheelchair on those trips to the kennel. This was intended to create a diversion and a false sense of dependence to those around him.

Chapter 40

Grey clouds danced around us and left droplets of sleet on my red parka. Jake pushed Patrick over the pebbled walkway to the training center. Nickie and I were off leash. We ran through the leafy area leading to the double wooden doors. Nickie had a funny habit I liked to watch. He'd hold his face straight up, then bite as the droplets of sleet landed on his black wet nose. In the meantime, his black curly coat would be covered with sleet. He'd give himself a tremendous shake and off it would fly. Oh, how my new puppy pal loved the cold.

Patrick and Nickie would have an hour of workout with Miss Robin, now an accepted teacher in my view. She taught Patrick hand commands so he could follow through with her training.

Jake walked back outside from the kennel to the brick building where he joined the poker game already in play. I bolted ahead as fast as my short legs could travel to get out of the sleet. I preferred the warmth provided me under the table. J.D. was at his usual seat as dealer.

I hoped the agents were parked someplace close. They'd said they would be in a utility truck ready to record the info from Jake's wire. My ears were alert, ready for some incriminating evidence. I laid quietly watching shoes and socks cross and uncross as the men sitting above me played their poker hands.

I heard nothing about jewelry stores or robberies. Mr. Cohen's name was not discussed even though Jake brought it up a couple times when talking about the training center. If they knew any facts, they sure weren't talking.

In the dimly lit room, I recognized all the players. Over to the side sat Mr. Sunglasses. He'd always been in the kitchen, to do business, to act as cashier. He sat, reading and exchanging chips for money. His voice was muffled. Contrary to most people I'd been around, I had no clear understanding of his words.

Talk was at a minimum until Patrick came in. The game broke up for a few minutes, the players got a little more talkative and took bathroom breaks. They asked how he was doing. How his dog was working out. Those kinds of questions. Nothing said was worth wearing a wire for. All turned quiet as they sat down to play another game. I may have dozed a little. After what could have been either a short or a long time, I jumped wide awake when someone's fist hit the table. Cowboy had, to quote, "won myself a heap of moo-lay."

Patrick turned to Jake and said, "I'm not feeling well. Could you drive me home? Sorry, guys, I need to call it a day."

No one seemed to mind. Jake rolled him to the training center. We picked up Nickie, loaded the SUV, and were out of there. Today's plan had been a huge disappointment.

On the drive home, Nickie jumped in and laid down taking up the back seat. I decided it was time to teach him that I was the alpha dog. I started with a low snarl, progressed to a deeper growl. Nickie sat straight up in the back seat. His piercing black eyes were wide with shock as he watched me. Then I added a fierce bark. That did the trick. Nickie jumped down to the floorboard and laid there for the ride home. On our next 'GO' trip I'll let him sit on the seat with me. I may be a little in size compared to him, but that doesn't mean I can't become ferocious. I think he got the drift.

From the front seat I heard the guys talk. "We weren't getting anything. I thought it best to leave." Patrick said. "You noticed, I made sure I'd lost a pot so leaving would not create any problem."

"Yeah, I picked up on that. Cowboy was in seventh heaven with that pot. It was like no one would say anything other than talk about your dog," said Jake. "I felt like we were in a silent movie."

Patrick said, "I agree. It was pretty obvious after today's game, there would be nothing more than small talk while we're playing."

"I'll call the agents when we get in and tell them. Their idea isn't going to work. You need any help getting in?"

"No, I like leaving the wheelchair upstairs in the hall. I don't feel like I'm improving as fast as I'd like. Still, I try using the walker around the loft."

I had a feeling deep in my dog brain, my sweet Momma would have a plan when she heard about today's failure to get information. She was in the kitchen when we got home. Jake told her about the Agents' botched plan as he brought their grilled cheese to the table.

Grilled cheese is a close second to my favorite foods, steak, raw if you please, and asparagus. I followed Jake from the stove to the table when I saw the melted cheese running from the bread slices. Jake took his seat at the table and, just as I expected, he slipped me a bite.

Izzie followed carrying bowls of steaming tomato soup. I wasn't so lucky with Momma. As she tore a corner of her grilled cheese, her wrist bumped her soup bowl. Tomato soup spread over the table the speed of a mud slide. Paper towels to the rescue.

They finished their lunch deciding Jake, per Hannah's request, would drive Patrick to his Orthopedics' appointment tomorrow. They still had time to make other plans with the agents. I went to bed right after my night-time nature call. What a day it had been. Worthless.

Momma had a decision to make tomorrow.

Chapter 41

I woke Friday morning before the sky was light to the sound of tiny rodent feet as they scurried across the kitchen floor. Quietly, I left my bed and headed for the kitchen in time to see my arch nemesis nibbling a bagel crumb. He starred at me with his beady eyes then darted under the sink cabinet. That little devil had a new hole, a new hiding place. If I ever catch the little shit, I'll show no mercy.

Buddy and Daisy followed me into the kitchen and headed for their water bowls. Dejected, I followed.

Izzie strolled into the kitchen, all happy smiles, wearing her red sweats and humming *Rudolf the Red Nosed Reindeer*. Jake gathered his robe around him as he made coffee. He poured Izzie and himself a cup as his phone rang. He answered, frowned, ran his fingers through his hair as he hung up. "What's the chance of you driving Patrick and Nickie today?"

"Sure, what's wrong?"

"That call was our ranch neighbor to the north. He said the Mississippi was rising fast. We've got cattle in the bottoms. I need to get down there, get a couple of the hands and load the horses. It'll take some time to drive the herd to high ground."

"I was going to talk to you about today's training session anyway."

"What about today's session?"

"Never mind. It's not that important. You go on, we'll talk tonight."

"I'll go as soon as I finish this. We could be late getting in tonight. Don't wait up."

Jake finished his scrambled eggs and sausage, then hurried down the hall to get dressed. Buddy followed.

There was a manliness about the way Jake strode into a room, the way he stood tall. His mannerisms gave me confidence he was there for us. For a few moments he leaned against the kitchen counter, arms folded, watching Izzie. Then he walked to her, touched her cheek and kissed her. He turned toward the front door, grabbed his coat and said, "Let's go, pal." Buddy's tail wagged briskly as he ran to follow Jake out the door.

The wind turned cold overnight. It howled as we enjoyed our morning outing in the courtyard. There was no squirrel to be seen.

The rest of the morning Momma wrapped presents and ran to the bathroom several times. I'd noticed she did that frequently. I don't mind telling you I was more than upset when I realized the new baby was the cause of Momma's bathroom trips. It was already causing problems for my Sweet Momma. I didn't know why she needed someone else in our lives.

Sweet Momma left Princess Daisy with Hannah when we drove Patrick and Nickie to the kennels. We loaded the wheelchair and took off at neck breaking speed.

Patrick hooked his seat belt and turned to Momma. "I'm getting a little tired of depending on you folks driving every time we go to the kennels," he said.

"I know, but your cover is for everyone there to think you're in worse shape than you are. Anyway, after today it may be over."

"Do you have everything the Agents gave you? I was a little surprised they agreed with your idea when you met them yesterday at their office. What did Jake say?"

"I didn't tell him. He left in such a hurry to move cattle, I saw no reason to worry him."

"You know he'd be worried sick if he knew your plan. He'd never approve of this after the scare you gave him on the cruiser."

"Well, ignorance is bliss is my motto," said Izzie as she whipped the car off the highway and started up the drive to the kennels.

Chapter 42

In the smoky, dim lit room, I recognized all the players but did not see Mr. Sunglasses. He'd always been in the kitchen, sitting, reading and exchanging chips for money. If he were somewhere in the darkened room I didn't see or hear him. I did hear his voice the day he went outside to talk to some guy, but his voice was muffled so I had no clear understanding of his conversation.

Today, as he puffed on a vile smelling cigar, J.D. handled the cashier duties as well as being dealer.

It was probably best he wasn't there. Perfect for Izzie to carry out the new scheme for collecting information. Momma knew better than to ask if she could join the men. Since she couldn't play Texas Holdem' she got Patrick settled at the table, then we went to the kennels to watch Nickie have his lesson. Momma sat in the bleachers with her big purse beside her. I rested my bottom at her feet.

I was amazed Nickie was such a good student. He responded to every sit, down, and stay command Miss Robin told him. I thought he was finished, then she gave him all sorts of hand commands. It was amazing what Nickie could do and he was still a puppy.

I was beginning to understand the hand commands when Momma stirred in her seat, looked at her watch and said to Miss Robin, "We need to leave soon. Is Nickie about finished for today?"

"Sure. Just give me a couple minutes to wind down this set."

Momma tugged her purse over her shoulder, handed us both a treat and took Nickie's leash in her hand with mine. We headed on the path covered with crunchy leaves toward the brick building with the black windows. Nickie did pull on his leash when Patrick first got him, but he learned that lesson well. Now he paraded like a soldier.

The holly trees swayed back and forth. Mr. Wind blew strong and fierce. Only one motorcycle was parked by the building that day.

Momma opened the door revealing the room hazy from the cigar smoke. She must have been surprised by the dimness. She stepped over the threshold but not high enough. She stumbled caught herself on the door frame but dropped Nickie's leash. He ran straight to Patrick and the group. The confusion that followed disrupted the game, but the men didn't seem to mind. Momma said to Patrick, "If you've got him, maybe I need to use the little girls room before we leave."

"You take your time. This young scamp's just fine," said red beard as he gave Nickie's huge neck a firm rubbing and spit in his Campbell can.

"Come on, Sam, with me. Those guys don't need to have two of you running loose."

Knowing she was free to go to the bathroom meant she was also free to walk around the dark room. Perfect for her to carry out her plan. This plan, she told me in the restroom, was to get information using microphones. "In other words, Sammy. We're bugging this place." With a wink in my direction she closed the restroom door behind us and headed for the kitchen area. As we walked between the bookshelves, she hurriedly placed one of the little black microphones under a bookshelf.

With Mr. Sunglasses gone we were free to move around, but Momma's actions made my heart pump against my ribs. I knew it was time to get out of there. I ran toward the door and barked my loudest bark. This was my distraction so the guys would look at me at the door and not toward Momma as she slid the black box under the lip of the kitchen counter.

Leaving got more confused when Momma let Nickie's leash get caught in the wheel of Patrick's wheelchair. I try not to use the word klutz, but—

I am sure about one thing. Those poker-playing guys were glad to get rid of us even if Patrick did pick up a couple thousand. Izzie laughed when he told her about his winnings as we drove home.

"At least there wasn't a failure on one count," she said.

We pulled in the garage to see a mechanic over by Olivia's parking slot. Izzie drove closer and saw the guy from Paul's Repair was working on the motorcycle, not in her slot but in the one next to hers. Patrick said, "Looks like the guy in 1-B's got a problem. I'd noticed an oil leak there last week. Guess he had to hire someone to fix it."

Izzie opened the back-car door for us to jump out. I'll say this for Nickie, he remembered my lesson to let me jump out first. He was a giant of a pup. Still, he was learning to follow my adult teaching. Otherwise he could've squashed me. I ran over to Miss Leona, who was starting to unload a sack of groceries. I was one thought ahead of Nickie, 'cause I knew what she always kept in her car. True to my memory she came through for us with a tasty treat. I gave her the big eye look with a fast tail wag as my thank you. Nickie, who by then, stood above Miss Leona's knees, followed my action. He was a fast learner.

"Hey, Leona, how you and Harry doing? Are you ready for the holidays?" Izzie yelled. "It looks like Mr. Devilin has some problems."

"We're doing great. Got our tree today. Yes, I talked to Mr. Devilin this morning after he called the mechanic. He was upset because he was going to miss an important meeting, someplace he was supposed to be this afternoon."

His reaction to the problem seemed kind of dumb to me. Wondered why he didn't call a cab. Maybe he didn't want anyone to know where the meeting was taking place.

Chapter 43

We stepped off the elevator into a dark bleak hallway. No light meant Momma needed to call Mr. Harry to put in a new bulb. Patrick's walker was leaning against the wall. He used it as he led Nickie into their unit. We walked toward ours. I was exhausted, I needed a drink of water and a nap.

Momma approached the lock with her key, but our door was ajar. It's not like her to leave the door unlocked. Were we in a hurry this morning when we left? There is a second exit door from her bedroom into the hall, but we never go out that way. No, we exited the same way we always do, through the front.

Momma remained calm a she turned the doorknob to push the door open. I ran inside like I always do and headed for my water bowl. Wow, the kitchen was a mess. Drawers pulled out. Utensils on the floor. I turned in time to see Momma walking, unaware of the kitchen turmoil, toward her bedroom. I ran to warn her there was a problem, but I was too late.

I found her in the middle of her bedroom, unable to move, rubbing the nape of her neck. Pillows were off the bed, the mattress was off sideways with a slit in several places. Drawers were pulled out and turned over. She wrapped her arms around herself and rocked from side to side. We had a problem. We'd had an intruder. Or, did we still have an intruder?

I knew exactly why Momma was motionless, locked in place. I knew the story she'd told me when I still had a lot of energy in my step. At the time Momma was a teenager, she played with the marching band at the high school football games. On the evening in question, Momma came home to an empty house because her parents were still at the game. She'd left the game a little before the final play with a friend who dropped her off at the front door so she could change for the homecoming dance.

She went upstairs to her room, undressed out of her band uniform which she laid on her bed. She put on her new purple and white sweater dress to wear to the homecoming dance. All she needed were her purple suede shoes from the shoe rack in her closet.

She walked the length of her bedroom toward her closet. She reached out, turning the doorknob to open the closet door and tripped on a scatter rug on the slippery oak floor. Down she went. At the same moment, a male figure burst from the closet, dressed in black with a knife in his hand. She saw him swing the knife at her as she fainted. He must have been as scared as she because he ran. She awoke to find her friend kneeling beside her.

When the police interviewed her, they said the intruder had escaped through the upstairs hall window dropping to a roofed deck below. They thought he choose the window, thinking her parents were downstairs.

I knew Momma was reliving that past history with an intruder as she stood there. This is the only time I can be for sure in saying, Izzie being a klutz probably saved her life.

Momma looked down at me and rushed forward. "Come on, Love Sponge."

We ran across the hall. Momma beat on Hannah's door. It took several minutes for it to open. Hannah opened it and Izzie staggered as she fell into her sister's arms. "Someone's in or has been in my house. Everything's a mess," she shrieked. "Call the police. Please. Now."

Patrick listened to what was said, went in the kitchen, and opened a drawer. He came back to where we stood and stepped around the girls as he leaned on his walker. I saw a '32 sticking in his back waist as he hobbled out the door. Nickie's protective nature kicked in. He followed close to Patrick's side as they headed across the hall. I could not help but notice Patrick still had a deep limp.

While we waited for the police, Hannah fixed Momma some hot tea and handed me a piece of raw-hide. Daisy welcomed me, not knowing the problem Momma and I had experienced. For once, I was too shaken for any dog-speak. I gnawed on my raw-hide instead.

Patrick walked in, wide-eyed in disbelief. He described the conditions he'd seen. First, the kitchen. A mess I was well aware of. Second, the living room. Several cushions were slashed with stuffing everywhere. Only a few drawers opened, some on the floor, one turned upside down. Third, the bedroom. Utter chaos. I realized that meant the person was in the loft while we were there. I lay on Hannah's tile kitchen floor trembling.

"When you and Sammy came to our place the intruder had enough time to check out the living room before the cops got there. He probably took a fast look around before running out," Patrick said.

I thought of an idea and ran out Hannah's loft down the hall to the Exit door. Sure enough, it was partway open. Thanks Perry.

Chapter 44

Daisy and Nickie had called it a day and gone to bed by the time Jake and Buddy arrived home that night. Jake found everything in the loft in turmoil. He came across the hall to check out what happened. His clothes were filthy. He carried muddy boots in his hand. I could tell by the dark circles around his eyes that he'd had a hard day driving cattle. But, true to the Jake I knew, and Izzie loved, he handled the situation carefully, suggesting to Hannah and Patrick that he and Momma should stay with them that night.

He said he would shower then begin the work of putting the loft back in order. His sweetheart did not need to go through this tonight. On second thought, neither did he. A new mattress would need to be bought. Cleaning off the powder used to get fingerprints would take time. Too much for tonight. Jake looked fresher when he walked back in Hannah's unit. He grabbed sweet Momma around the waist, planting a big kiss on her.

It was good we were all staying the night with Hannah and Patrick. Staying with them kind of eased the tension from the situation that came up next. Jake listened as Izzie told about planting the 'bugs' in the gambling room. The more she told, the more red his face got.

Jake blurted to Izzie. "How could you do such a dumb thing? Did it ever dawn on you those men are dangerous criminals, not good old boys in for a game of poker?"

"I discussed it with the agents yesterday when you took Patrick to the doctor. They thought planting the mic was better than wearing a wire. I meant to tell you, but things got away from me."

"Got away from you? I know better than that. You could have told me that this morning before I left to move the cattle, before you drove Patrick out there."

"I was supposed to ask you to do it but when I knew the river was rising and the cattle had to get moved from the bottoms, I thought it best to just do it myself," Izzie said.

Jake shook his head as he ran his fingers through his black wavy hair. His square jaw usually formed a slight smile. Not that night. He was angry and it showed. As the night wore on, he and Patrick hashed out everything about the bugs at the kennel. I was too tired to listen. My eyes drooped, but I caught the next thing that happened.

Jake turned, with a faint smile, he looked at Momma, leaned over, brushed back her hair and kissed the top of her head. With a familiar gleam in his eye, he said, "If I didn't love you so much I wouldn't be worried about you, Sweetheart."

She shifted her weight, stretched her arms out to catch and embrace him. All was well. I crept next to Nickie and lay beside him. I needed some comforting myself.

After they finished talking about the episode in their loft, everyone settled down. No one had any idea who, or even how this could have happened. Hannah, though home all day, had heard nothing regarding a break-in. She said she and her tummy slept most of the day.

"In the morning I'll go to the store for some more cleaning supplies. Maybe pick up an oven roasted chicken to save cooking for a few meals," Izzie said as they walked arm in arm down Hannah's hall to the guest bedroom.

The day ended well.

Chapter 45

Izzie hummed *Jingle Bells* as she opened the car door for me and Daisy to jump in. Daisy went first. I'd stopped. Something was not right. Before I saw anyone, I smelled the leathery, musky, woody scent. Aramis. I smelled him. I smelled fear. For a moment I froze in place. Panic grabbed me. Unable to loosen its grasp, I turned.

There he stood. Uncle Jessie, Jerry Devilin, the devil himself. He removed his sunglasses. Momma did not see the dark figure that had slowly approached us.

Instead Momma glanced down at me. She waited for me to jump in behind Daisy. My hair bristled. Momma stepped back and turned to be face-to-face with the person she was terrified of. Her mouth twisted as if to speak but she said nothing as she gazed wide-eyed at the hooded man who approached her.

"Stay right where you are, young lady. Don't move," said her thought-to-be-dead uncle. He pushed back the hood of his black sweatshirt revealing a scared left jaw and ear.

Izzie straightened, squaring her shoulders as she stared him down. He came closer. "Why would I move?" Momma said. "I've been wondering if it were true, that, you did escape the explosion. I'll say this, your surgeon did a masterful job on your face. It took me a few seconds to recognize it was you."

"Of course, I'm alive despite what you've put me through. Saying I blew up your cruiser. Accusing me of murdering my brother and all. Every problem in this family goes back to that stupid letter your dumb-ass nanny wrote. She was the cause of all our family problems. Stupid bitch. Well, I took care of that problem."

"I knew you did it," Izzie said.

"Had to be done. Then she goes and somehow gets that letter to you after she's dead. My precious Hannah, my only child, was put through so much just because that bitch ratted on me."

"So, you say your killings were the fault of Clarabelle?"

"Not the killings. I had to take care of your mother. My brother was mean to her. I'd watched them through the years, she told me how he acted when he was drunk. It got to me. I had to give her some peace."

"Peace. You callous bastard. We were a happy family before daddy was killed."

Jessie stepped closer. I showed him my teeth and snarled. He looked down but kept talking. "You were the youngest. Sure, you thought everyone was happy. You had no idea what went on in that house."

"I was a happy child."

"Yes, I'd say you were happy with your dad. Hannah was happiest with her mother. Course she never knew it was all because she was my child, not my brothers. You never knew the heartache your mother felt. Through all those years, she confided in me. I could not stand to hear of what she went through married to him. I've loved her since the first day I met her at her eighteenth birthday party."

"That's what you call love? Give me a break. You're repulsive."

"You think so, huh? You don't realize, I know how to show my love.

You wouldn't say I'm repulsive if you'd seen the diamond I gave Olivia for Christmas."

"Wait a minute. You were connected to Mr. Cohen." Momma paused. "You murdered him. You probably got her ring at a jewelry heist."

"That Cohen, son-of-a-bitch, set me up, wouldn't pay me, said I owed him. After the games I handled for him. That guy would've taken my soul if he could've."

"That is if you had one to give. I bet you started the fire in his loft too."

"Nay, not me. It was some stupid painter from the construction crew. I'd never hurt anything of Hannah's."

Izzie hesitated before answering. "Wait a minute. Are you the Jay Mother's been talking about? Were you the one with her at the masquerade party?"

"I'm the one." he smirked.

"All those planned get-togethers when mother was bringing her friend, Jay, were just a set-up. She was talking about you, right? You were in my home."

"Back then and again yesterday. I will admit, I enjoyed seeing your lovely loft decorated for Christmas. I had reason to go through your house. I want, I need that damn letter. Just give it to me and we'll be fine. We're family. All will be forgiven."

"Who's forgiving who? How did you know I was gone yesterday?"

"Well, Little Lady, yesterday when I couldn't drive my Harley out to the kennels, I was here to see you leave with Patrick. It was the perfect time to check out your loft for Clarabelle's letter."

"Wait a minute. Are you the Mr. Devilin who rented 1-B? How'd you know it was vacant? Oh, no. No. You didn't."

"Ah, not really difficult to do. She liked to visit with me, the FedEx man. Drop a drug in her coke bottle and she got pretty dozy. Then we talked. Her pillow sure came in handy. Not a loss. She was in her eighties. Time to meet her maker. I'd say, she sure thought a lot about the FedEx guy, we had some good conversations before the last one."

"You're also the man Jake said oversaw the Texas-Hold'em games? Right?"

"One and the same," he laughed.

I pushed against Momma's leg and growled. She kept talking.

"Oh, my goodness. You've been around for months. How'd you get up to the fourth floor without being seen? When did you use the elevator?"

"Easy-peasy. When you were gone last summer, I was visiting Avi Greenbacks, Abram Cohen to you, most every day, even stayed a couple nights till we came to a tragic misunderstanding. Anyway, thinkin' I might need to visit you all at a later date I jammed the exit door. That was one smart move, if I do say so. Sure, came in handy yesterday."

As he talked, Izzie opened the back door. Still growling, I jumped in and hopped into my doggie seat. Momma put her hand on the front door handle. Jessie took a quick step toward the car, putting his hand on hers.

I stood tall and brave, and barked my meanest bark.

She could not open the car door.

Jessie was less smug and more nasty as he leaned in toward Izzie and stared directly into her eyes, "Now, get this. I need that letter. This little game can go easy or not. It all depends on you, Little Lady. All I want is that letter and no one gets hurt."

"How about Patrick? He's already been hurt."

"Let me tell you about him. I didn't like my daughter marrying a man whose family, Clarabelle, spilled-the-beans on me. I couldn't stop the wedding, but I can sure as hell make his life miserable. Maybe, eliminate him completely if he causes my Hannah any trouble. Blood's thicker un' water, they say. He might turn on her any day. We'll discuss more about him tomorrow, same time, same place when you bring Clarabelle's letter.

"Oh, I forgot. I'll be seeing you for dinner tonight at your place. Best for you to forget this little chat took place. Olivia said you wanted us to come over to draw names for Christmas. Your mother understands me. She knows I've worshiped her since we were kids. She doesn't hold me accountable for the murders. Don't judge her, Little Lady."

He smirked, "It's so nice to have family around during the holidays."

Before she could collect herself and put the key in the ignition, Jessie jumped on his Harley. He gunned the engine and took off, spinning the wheels as he drove out of the garage into the cold December air.

Sweet Momma sat at the wheel. She put her palms to her forehead. Her knuckles were white as she gripped the steering wheel, her eyes stared into space. What to do next. She opened the car door for Daisy and me, let us run to the courtyard to do our business, then herded us toward the elevator.

There was nothing Momma could do. She needed to share this with Jake, Hannah and Patrick. We found Jake in the kitchen. Sweet Momma was so shaken she stumbled forward. Jake turned toward us in time to catch her. In short gasps Momma told him some of what had happened. Jake was not a calm person. He paced the floor, then called Patrick and Hannah to come over. They all began a long conversation over steaming coffee and bagels.

Chapter 46

Izzie collapsed on the sectional and drew her legs up under her. I jumped up beside her, she hugged me close as a frown crossed her forehead. Then she rubbed the nape of her neck as she began to tell what happened earlier.

Momma said she went to the garage with me and Daisy for a trip to Kroger. Daisy jumped in the car, but I wouldn't. She was unaware someone was watching her until he was about two car lengths away. She said when I refused to jump in the car that should have been a clue, knowing how I always respond to 'GO'.

"Jessie was wearing a black hoodie so, at first I didn't recognize him. Then he started talking, accusing Clarabelle as being the real problem. He said she had fabricated the story in her letter telling us he killed daddy."

"Is he crazy?" Patrick said.

"I believe he was trying to justify his actions. Eluding to, yet not fully admitting, he'd murdered our father, Clarabelle, and Mr. Cohen. There was, in his mind, a reason these people had to be eliminated."

"Weren't you scared?" Hannah asked.

"For some reason, I wasn't," Izzie answered. "At least, not at first. Then, toward the end he became more insistent about getting the letter Clarabelle wrote us. He glared at me. Then, I was frightened."

"I'd have gotten out of there," Hannah said.

"Right. I tried, but he forced the car door shut to finish his warning. Sammy was getting upset. Growling and showing his teeth. I was really nervous."

Momma told how Jessie finally released his hold on the car handle, then sped away on his Harley.

"What do we do now?" asked Hannah. "Call the police?"

"We'd better call the Feds first. They need to know Jessie has shown himself. He said he was coming here tonight with Mother," Momma said.

"Do you think he will?" asked Jake.

"Considering his past record, I'd say no. But now he seems more daring, more determined to have a showdown to get Clarabelle's letter."

Jake said, "He might just show up with Olivia to test our reactions. I say, wait, let's not call anyone just yet - see if he shows tonight."

Chapter 47

That evening, the night Jessie referred to, was the night the family planned to be together for dinner and draw names for Christmas. Nickie came over with his parents and ate his supper with Buddy, Daisy, and me. Izzie and Hannah cooked. The tangy smell I picked up on was coming from the dill sauce Hannah was stirring as the finishing touches for the salmon. Without the dill, salmon is a great tasty food, next to a steak, raw, if you please, and asparagus. Why my family wanted to mess up good salmon taste with butter and dill is beyond me. Keep it plain for me.

Momma moved aimlessly as she fixed those terrible fishy prawns. She always served those shrimp-like fish with the sauce that cleans out my nose when I smell it. Momma once called it horseradish. Another example of unrealistic human words. Horses we all know like carrots, but radishes, I don't think so. At one time I considered the word to mean a radish as big as a horse. That made even less sense. As I've aged, I've learned to forget it. I don't like cocktail sauce because of the horseradish, and I doubt there is a horse alive who likes it either.

The gals finished their cooking chores and retired to the living room. No one was talking, perhaps lost in their own thoughts. With the back of her left hand, Hannah wiped her nose from the bubbles I could see popping from her glass of ginger ale. Izzie sat with her legs tucked under her, sipping her glass of sparking water. . The guys poured amber liquid from the XXX Reserve bottle, joined the sisters, sitting in recliners with their feet elevated. Hannah leaned back against two pillows the color of a Tennessee sunset over the Mississippi.

Our Christmas tree sparkled with hundreds of tiny white lights. Yet, it did nothing to give a glint of happiness to my loved ones. Other than Izzie occasionally running to the bathroom, everyone sat still, waiting for their guests.

A knock on the door brought Izzie to her feet. I was at her heels running to greet Olivia, afraid her guest might appear this time. Izzie opened the door expecting to see her mother. There stood Miss Leona with a cell phone in her hand.

"Your Mothers just called me. She's been trying to reach you and Hannah. Hannah didn't answer. Your phone, she said, just rang and rang. Are you okay? Do you need to use my phone?"

"Rats, no, thank you, I put my phone on vibrate earlier when I took a nap. I never turned it back on. I'm so sorry you had to come up. Hannah's here, probably left her phone in the apartment. I'll call Mother now."

"Please do. She was very excited and crying, I think. She didn't say what was wrong, seemed panic-stricken, her voice was hysterical. Let me know if you need me to help in any way."

"I will. Thanks again." Sweet Momma shut the door so fast I didn't get my usual pat from Miss Leona. Bummer. Momma frowned as she turned to face her family.

She walked back into the living area. "Did you all hear that? I'd better call Mother now."

Hannah adjusted one of her pillows and said, "Will you please put the call on speaker so we can all hear? No need to try to explain. God only knows what has upset her this time."

"Will do. Hello, Mother. Leona was just here. Sorry you couldn't reach us. What's wrong? We thought you'd be here by now. We've poured drinks and your favorite prawns are chilled."

"I declare, Izzie," Olivia snapped through gasping breaths, "haven't I taught you there are more important things in life than what you eat?"

"What, well, yes, I know there are more important things in life than prawns. They were being served especially for you and your guest. Is that so wrong? So, get on with it. What's the matter?"

"Don't you be snappy with me, young lady. Let me talk to your sister. She'll at least talk civil to her mother. She's always had a more humane soul than you ever thought about."

Izzie held her phone out to her sister, tears forming in Sweet Momma's reddening eyes.

"Hello, Mother, sweetheart, how can we help?" Hannah said in the syrupy, unnatural voice saved only for her mother.

"Oh, my sweet girl, I'm at the hospital. He's been hurt, nearly killed. I've been so happy these past few months. Now this, oh, whatever will I do if I lose him this time."

"Who, Mother? What happened? Do you need us to come?

"It's Jay, dear. He was riding his Harley to meet me when a tire blew, throwing him under a car. I saw it all happen right before my eyes. Oh, dear, oh dear. He's in surgery now. You can understand. You've been through sudden tragedy. Can you leave Patrick with them and come help see me through this?

Yes, I'll drive right there now, okay?"

"Great. You can tell Izzie to eat those darn prawns herself."

Hannah grabbed her coat and hurried toward the front door. Izzie picked up her phone and dialed. "Hello, Is this the IRS Central Office? May I speak to Agent—

At that precise moment I heard the running of tiny rodent feet, but I knew what was important in my life. I ran to my sweet Momma who was now nestled against Jake's shoulder. I jumped in her lap. My doggie instinct said, "All is well."

I wagged my tail. Tap. Tap. Tap

THE END

Epilogue

PRISONER ESCAPES HOSPITAL
David King
Memphis Commercial Times
USA TODAY NETWORK – Tennessee

n escape, yesterday, December 24, 5:45 CST, from the Elvis Presley Trauma Center-Regional One Health Medical Center has the Memphis City Police on high alert.

The fugitive, Jessie DeLisle, alias Jerry Devilin, escaped from police custody while being transported to the West Wing of the facility. This area of the Center is still on lock-down as we go press.

According to Memphis police, fugitive DeLisle had been hospitalized December 20 due to a motorcycle accident in which he involved. The hit and run occurred on Osborn Street, North of Riverside Drive.

DeLisle underwent surgery and was in recovery when arrested December 21. Although under police guard, he managed to escape during transportation.

Police investigators, at the time of this report, are baffled by the disappearance. DeLisle is reported to be dangerous and violent.

Residents in areas close to the Center are asked to be vigilant and on high alert for DeLisle. If he is spotted do not try to apprehend. Call 9-1-1 and state your location.

Thank You

Dear Reader,

Thank you for taking the time to read Dog Daze of Fall. If you enjoyed it, please consider telling your friends and posting a short review. Word of mouth is an author's best friend, helps more than you could possibly know, and is much appreciated.

About the Author

When Maryanne VanDyke started a book club in Southern Illinois fifty years ago, she never dreamed she would write her debut novel at the age of eighty-two.

Although VanDyke was a free-lance writer for the Evansville Courier in Evansville, Indiana and, later, for the City of Phoenix employee Newsletter, she had never written fiction. In 1995 she moved to Bella Vista, Arkansas and joined the Village Writing School in Eureka Springs. Under their tutorage she quickly began a southern adult mystery novel as told from the point of view of her Shih Tzu, Sam.

Upon moving to Smyrna, Tennessee, she joined a creative writing class at the Senior Center where she continued to embrace her mantra – repotyourlife – believing change to be the initial step toward growth no matter what your age.

VanDyke lives with Sam the Shih Tzu in Smyrna, Tennessee. Writing has become her passion as she consults with her furry super sleuth for the next three novels in their Dog-Tail Detective Series. When not writing, she teaches Mah Jongg and works at her new business venture, The Tipsy Concierge. Sam is rarely far from her lap.

Reach her on Facebook: Maryanne VanDyke, Author or maryannevandykeauthor@gmail.com

Made in the USA
Monee, IL
08 June 2020

32672534R00098